ALL TIED UP FOR NEW YEAR'S

PATRICIA D. EDDY

JUST FOR YOU

Do you want inside news on sales, new releases, and giveaways? Just sign up for my mailing list on my website: http://patriciadeddy.com.

A favor...

After you finish this book, you'd make my day if you'd take a few moments to leave a review and tell your friends about All Tied Up For New Year's. You can leave a review where you purchased the book and on Goodreads.

1

Elora

*M*y ass hits the cement and the air leaves my lungs in a violent hiccup, tears burning the corners of my eyes. Shame heats my cheeks as the perfectly-wrapped jewelry boxes tumble out of my bag and over the snow, their corners quickly soaking through. I should know better. I do know better. Winter in Boston, with its icy sidewalks and freak snow storms can be dangerous for anyone—let alone someone who can only see out of one eye. Add in a snowplow that hurtles frigid icicles toward you at light speed on a brilliantly sunny day, and boom! Disaster.

"Oh my God, are you all right?" A woman rushes over, golden hair swinging free, a long, leather coat brushing her calves. She kneels in the slush, resting a gloved hand on my shoulder. "Say something."

"F-fine," I offer once my breath returns. I feel more stupid than injured, though the man she's with extends a hand to help me up, and I wince as I try to get my feet under me. I can't read the emotion in his brown eyes, but his full lips curve into a frown, and he sidesteps me. Strong hands cup my elbows as he sets me to rights again, and I catch a whiff of his scent. Spicy aftershave, not too much, leather, and something that reminds me of home. I turn slightly so I can get a better look at him and almost lose my words at his angular jaw, the muscles obviously bulging under his wool coat. "Th-Thank you," I stammer as I try not to drool.

Once I'm upright, I meet Elizabeth Bennett's gaze, and I'm in serious danger of gawking—again. "Are you hurt?" she asks, her voice kinder, more caring than I expect. Her dark-clad companion retrieves my packages, brushing the snow off each one before carefully tucking them into my bag.

"I don't think so." I try to help, but my boot catches another patch of ice, and I skid into Elizabeth, sending us both careening into a parked car. "Son of a motherless goat!"

"Go inside," the man—who is definitely not her fiancé, body-guard maybe?— says with a deep, firm voice I could probably listen to all day long. "I'll retrieve your things." His accent reminds me of Greece, and as he picks up the next box, his dark gaze seeks me out. Elizabeth takes my arm, but I'm paralyzed by his stare—not to mention the rest of him. Six-foot-four if he's an inch, at least two hundred pounds, with cheekbones from the gods and a square jaw dusted with stubble, he sends my heart racing and I don't even know his name.

Elizabeth clears her throat, and concern colors her tone. "Can you walk?"

"Usually. Today, the jury's still out." I let her help me into Artist's Grind, and the scent of coffee makes my mouth water. Devan only sells the very best beans, and I've been aching for a cup all morning. Elizabeth settles me at one of the bistro tables in the center of the small space. I give Devan a tentative wave as she chats with a customer at the register and nod at her boyfriend, Mac, when he sets a weighty bag of coffee beans on the counter.

"What do you want? The coffee's on me." Elizabeth holds out her hand with a warm smile. "I'm Elizabeth Bennett."

"I know." I try not to cringe at my gaffe, shake my head, and grip her fingers firmly. "I'm sorry. Elora Kalivas. I swear, my manners—and my balance—are usually better."

Laughing, Elizabeth gives my hand a final squeeze. "I've lived in Boston for seven years, and I still take at least one tumble every winter. Coffee fixes everything, and Devan makes the best pour-overs. Or are you a latte woman?"

I should protest. After all, I ran into her. But the fine Greek specimen—and I mean that literally: if he's not from Greece, I'll eat my winter coat—pulls open the door, stamps his feet to clear them of snow, and catches my eye. I can barely mumble, "Pour-over...whatever Devan recommends," before my mouth goes dry and my palms dampen inside my gloves.

Despite the problems with my right eye, the left works just fine, thank you very much, and I gawk as the Greek god sets my bag down next to me—a little damp, but otherwise intact. "You need better boots."

"What?" I barely register his words, so taken with his olive skin and dark eyes. And his voice. Let's not ignore that, shall we? How he rolls his r's, the roundness of his o's...I could listen to him all day. "Oh. Boots." I look down, and my cheeks catch fire. At least my complexion assures me I don't look as embarrassed as I feel. "I have some. I just...they're getting resoled, and this storm came out of nowhere." The boots aren't the problem. My traitorous body is. But he can't know about my issues. I don't *look* disabled. No one can tell the whole right side of my body is weak, that I suffer from seizures, that I'm blind in one eye. My iris is a little paler in my right eye, a little cloudy, but most people never notice. Or they stare, as if they can't quite figure out what's wrong with me.

He frowns, his trim brows drawn together, making a furrow I want to smooth away. "I know you."

"No, I don't think so." I'd remember meeting him before. Though if he's Greek... But seventeen years is a long time. Not to mention two surgeries, twelve inches less hair, and twenty extra pounds. Okay, twenty-five.

"Milos Sagona." He offers his hand, but before I respond, Elizabeth returns, balancing three cups of coffee in her hands. Milos accepts one with a nod and sits at the next table, between Elizabeth and the front door. His gaze never stills, flitting from patron to patron, the door, and Devan and Mac.

The scent of the coffee revives me and distracts me from my unbidden fantasies of Milos's arms around me. "There, that's better," Elizabeth says as she drops into a chair next to me. "Where were you headed all loaded down?"

"Here, actually." I motion to Devan and start to rise, but my right leg protests the effort. I guess I did a little more damage than I thought. Glancing at Elizabeth, I'm relieved she's too focused on her coffee to notice, but Milos...he's already half out of his seat when shake my head and lower myself back down. Great. *Of course* I'd meet a hot guy and have my body completely betray me. "Do you come here often?"

"Every chance I get. Though the past few months, I've been too busy. I finally told my fiancé I needed a day off from wedding planning. I swear the man has minions. Why can't they take over for a while?"

"Minions?" I can't help but laugh. "What did he say?" The idea that this woman speaks to Alexander Fairhaven—eats with Alexander Fairhaven, has sex with Alexander Fairhaven even— fills me with wonder. He's not my type—or at least, I don't think he is. The closest I've gotten to the man is knowing Devan and Mac. Earlier this year, Mac designed a sculpture for the lobby of the new Fairhaven Tower. A few stories were shared over a six-pack of beers one long, summer night. Stories I'll never repeat. Mac walked in on an office tryst in the middle of the installation. Even now, I fight my blush at the thought.

Elizabeth sips her drink and leans back in her chair, and I think I see a slight tremble to her fingers. "He offered to plan the whole damn thing himself. But that's even worse. The last time I told him to make a decision so I didn't have to, he called Vera Wang to design my dress. I could have fed a third-world country for the cost of that dress. I said no. Found the perfect dress at a second-hand shop on Houston Street. A few hours of alterations, and no one's ever going to know I didn't have it designed just for me." She beams with pride and fiddles with a diamond bracelet around her left wrist. A platinum lock secures the cuff, and I can't help but wonder if the rumors are true.

"The wedding's in less than a month, isn't it?" I thought I read something about a New Year's Eve ceremony and a grand ball. "What can you possibly have left to do?" I let my hair fall over my right eye and peer at the wealthy—and soon-to-be wealthier—woman cupping her mug like it contains the nectar of Heaven. I've seen her in the papers, but in person, she's lovelier. Fresher. Real. Of course, the Rock of Gibraltar on her ring finger chases a bit of that realism away, but tiny lines tighten around her lips, and her eyes are bloodshot. Up close, she looks like she needs a week at a spa. Or at least a good night's sleep.

"Only the most important thing ever." Elizabeth sighs and stares down at her hands. "I hate every wedding ring design the jeweler's come up with. They're all 'befitting a man of Alexander's station—and the woman he marries.' But they don't fit me."

"What do you want, then?" I speak the language, and I have a fair idea what a "man of Alexander's station" should want. I don't blame Elizabeth a bit for rejecting those designs. No personality. No heart.

A small smile graces her lips. "I want my grandmother's wedding ring. It's long gone now, or at least out of my reach, but..."

Devan rushes over and greets me with a hug and a kiss on the cheek. I hold onto her a little longer than usual, still kicking myself for ruining the gorgeous Christmas wrapping job on at least half of my wares. When I finally pull away, Devan's smiling, and I can't help responding in kind, even though my voice cracks a little as I gesture to the wilted bows and soaked corners. "The boxes got a little wet. But I'll bring some fresh ones down this afternoon once the ice melts."

"Oh hon, don't worry about that. I'll send Mac to walk you home, and he can cart them back, okay?"

I try not to show how much her offer means to me. I do okay most of the time. The headaches don't bother me more than once or twice a week, and I haven't had a seizure in a month. But a brief halo flashes behind Devan's brown curls, and I worry that run of good luck is soon to come to an end. I need to be careful today. "Thanks. Do you want me to arrange the display?" My voice drops to a whisper, and I hope she hears the plea behind my words.

"God, no. That's what you pay me the big bucks for. Elora makes jewelry, Elizabeth. Around the holidays, I have a hard time keeping her earrings in stock." Pride fills Devan's voice as she sweeps up the bag and practically dances off to the rear of the shop. With a practiced eye, Devan maneuvers some of the display racks full of scarves, mittens, stained glass art, hand-stamped stationary, and Mac's metal work.

"Really?" Longing lends a breathy sound to Elizabeth's tone, and her gaze bores into me, desperation darkening her blue eyes. "What kind?"

"Um, today I brought in six rings, a dozen pendants, five sets of earrings, and three bracelets. They're not fancy, but I enjoy working with my hands."

She looks down and gasps. "Oh my God. Did you make this?" Taking my left hand, she runs her index finger over the ring I wear on my thumb. The design resembles the gears on the Doctor's cradle from "A Good Man Goes to War," with a pale green peridot in the center. One of my first designs—I haven't removed the ring in ten years, other than for cleaning and my last surgery.

"Y-yes. One of my first pieces."

Elizabeth worries her lip between her teeth, still clutching my hand. "Could you...I mean...I know it's short notice, but..." Her eyes shimmer, and she glances over at Devan, who's draping several of my necklaces over Mac's metal sculptures, before returning her gaze to me. "My grandmother's ring wasn't stuffy and elegant and...polished. It was *real.* Like yours. It had character. Most of the wedding details I simply don't care about. I just want to marry Alexander. But the rings...these are symbols we'll wear for the rest of our lives..."

Hope lightens her face, so much that she seems to almost glow with excitement. "Elizabeth, I...I love what I do, but are you sure you shouldn't find a big-time designer? I can help you with some of the lingo if you'd like, but—"

"How quickly could you design me a ring? Or two? Could they be ready by New Year's Eve?"

I sputter, a bit of coffee sloshing over the rim of my mug. "I... um...yes? If we settled on a design in the next week or so... I brought a few other styles today if you want to look..."

Elizabeth beams and heads over to the display tables. My hip throbs as I push myself up to join her, and I curse my traitorous body, even as Milos takes my arm. "Careful," he says quietly. "The floor is wet."

Oh God. I'm half-tempted to fake a fall just to have his arms around me. Except Elizabeth oohs and ahhs over my designs, and I force myself to nod my thanks and then extract my arm from his warm grip. But since I can't tear my gaze from his, I bump into the table as I try to head for Elizabeth. "Shit." Forcing myself to look away, I chide myself. *He probably thinks you're drunk. At eleven in the morning. Great first impression, Elora.*

Elizabeth holds three of my rings. "These are so close. I love the—" she gestures with her free hand.

"Whorls."

"Yes, and the filigree. The inset on the middle one. And on this last one, the etching is gorgeous." She presses her lips together as she sets the rings back in their cases, then turns to me and swallows hard. "Can you combine all three of those looks and maybe a little bit of yours. In three weeks?"

Design a ring for a billionaire's wedding? The thought terrifies me, but Elizabeth's enthusiasm is infectious, and as she clutches my hand and pleads with me, I can't help but agree. "I have a sketchbook in my bag. I could rough out a couple of ideas for you now. Do you have a few minutes?"

"Absolutely. Let me call Alexander and tell him to cancel his meeting with Neil Lane. Thank God." She throws her arms around me and squeezes. "You're saving my wedding. Truly."

I highly doubt that, but still, I hug her back. After all, she—and her gorgeous hunk of a bodyguard—did prevent my ass from freezing to the sidewalk. I steal a glance at said gorgeous hunk, hovering close with a phone in his hand as I make my way to our table, and my cheeks flush.

"Elora Kalivas. I remember seeing you on television when I was young. The state dinner." His brows furrow, and he angles his head. "But after that, you disappeared. The papers spoke of rumors. The *vrykolakas* from Santorini. What really happened? Why did you leave Greece?"

Oh God. He knows. A flare of light draws my attention, but as soon as I turn my head, the brightness disappears. "Shit," I whisper as my messed-up brain decides now's the time to hit me with one of the cluster headaches that always precede a seizure. I've got ten minutes, maybe fifteen, before my body betrays me. Milos steadies me when I sway, and he tries to brush the hair away from the right side of my face.

"Are you all right, Elora?"

He says my name with such reverence, I fear his voice will drown me. I can't do this. I need my pills, my cat, and my bed.

8

Wrenching my arm free, I tug my bag over my shoulder. "Elizabeth, I'm sorry. I have to go. Now. My number's on the cards there. Call me tomorrow." With a last look into Milos's dark eyes, I flee, praying I'll reach my apartment without another fall.

Milos

Elizabeth stares after Elora, confusion pinching her brows. "Milos? What happened?"

I shift my focus to my boots and the drops of melted snow that gather around the chair. "I am sorry, Elizabeth. I spoke out of turn."

She arches a brow, and her voice takes on that authoritative tone she's picked up from Mr. Fairhaven—the one she uses on me when she thinks I'm being too hard on myself. "Sit. I think you need to tell me a little bit about Elora Kalivas. And how you know her."

Uncertainty churns in my gut as I fold my body into the small cafe chair across from Elizabeth. How much do I tell my employer about Greece's missing princess? Elora's card draws my gaze, and I run my fingers over the embossed lettering. The font fits her—so flowing and beautiful, yet still bold. "Years ago, back in Greece, the national papers claimed she was a vampire."

Elizabeth's eyes dance with her laughter, though she must see the sorrow written on my face, for she quickly stops. "A vampire. And people believed that?"

"Many of the small towns in my country...the old stories linger. A red-headed demon terrorizing the citizens. Children stolen in the night, blood painted on the doors. Few Greeks are born with red-hair. Elora...in the sun you can see the highlights.

Or, you could when she was a child. If pressed, most would admit there is no such thing as a *vrykolakas*, but a politician's daughter —well, it is much like in America. Those in the spotlight have targets on their backs."

"What happened to her?" She leans forward and rests her elbows on the table.

"I don't know the details. I was only seventeen when she disappeared from the public eye, and I enlisted in the military a month or two later. She made some sort of scene at a state dinner, and then her father lost the election. No one ever saw her after that." I shake my head. "Why did I remind her of that public shame?"

Though my words were meant more for myself than Elizabeth, she lays her hand on my arm. "Boot-in-mouth syndrome? Brought on by a sudden attraction to a beautiful woman?" Her understanding smile only serves to heighten my shame, and I pull away to stare into my coffee. "Milos, I'd have to be deaf not to hear how your voice changed when you spoke to her." She nudges the card towards me. "Call her. Apologize. Ask her out."

"I can't. She deserves better."

"Better?" Elizabeth snorts. "You saved my life. Alexander's life. You love your family, I've seen you stop the car to let ducks cross the road, and I'm pretty sure the last time I forced you to take a day off, you spent it volunteering down at the food bank. I don't know how much better of a man you could possibly be. Call. Her."

After more than a year of working for Alexander Fairhaven and protecting his fiancé, I've learned the futility of arguing with Elizabeth. Under her piercing gaze, I take the card and catch a whiff of Elora's perfume. Longing stirs deep inside, warming me in a way coffee never could, and I wonder, just for a moment, what she'd feel like pressed against me.

Until shame crushes those dreams into dust. I could be a much better man. Greece's princess deserves more than a killer.

Even if my crime did save two other lives. I'll call her because Elizabeth will hound me if I don't. But once I apologize, I'll walk away.

Flipping my coat collar up against the wind, I turn towards my apartment. After Elizabeth's former bosses had been sentenced, I'd no longer needed to live in the staff's quarters. Despite the proximity to my employer's ritzy neighborhood, this place is affordable. Though I've often wondered if Mr. Fairhaven had something to do with that. Scanning the street, I note the shadows, the hiding places, the potential threats. A hazard of my job.

Nights like this—the lightly falling snowflakes dancing on the breeze—always remind me of the shooting. Elizabeth's scream. Mr. Fairhaven's blood pooling, stark against the white backdrop of the snowy sidewalk. Carl's sightless eyes staring up at me. My mouth goes dry, and tension holds my head in a vise. Years in the Greek military prepared me to fight. They did not prepare me to kill. Not up close. Or rather, to forgive myself for killing. I had no choice. The assassin would have killed Elizabeth. Mr. Fairhaven spent days in the hospital and weeks recovering at home.

Yet, a year later, I still wake with the scent of gunpowder in my nose.

A letter from my mother waits in my mailbox. Even after I bought her a computer—and my sister taught her how to use email—she still writes to me. Climbing the steps to my door, I picture her huddled over her desk, painstakingly crafting every line. Once I pop a frozen burrito into the microwave, I tear open the card.

Dear Milos,

I hope you are well. Your father and grandmother send their love and hope you will be able to come home sometime next year. The vineyards are beautiful now that we have rented them to Mr. and Mrs. Elkenos. The profits are not high, but at least your father does not need to walk the hills every day.

Alesia and Doriana have talked of nothing but the big Christmas tree at Boston Commons and the ice skating. Will you be able to take us there when we visit?

Is there anyone special in your life? I worry about you, my son. More so around the holidays. What you went through last year...no one should have to carry that burden. You should be surrounded by love, not living alone, microwaving your food, with only television for company.

Please take care of yourself, Milos. The next few weeks will pass very slowly for me. Slower still because Dori asks me when we need to leave for the airport every few hours.

Love,

Mama

The microwave beeps, and I chuckle at Mama's telepathy. She has never been one to believe in the spiritual, but her letters are always eerily accurate, despite my best efforts to only let her see the good in my life.

As I sink down onto the couch with my dinner and a beer, something sharp pokes my leg. Elora's card. Running my finger over the embossed lettering, I wonder why Greece's fragile princess is hiding in the States. We only exchanged a few words, but I can't get her voice out of my head. Soft, yet strong. Her laughter as she spoke with Elizabeth, the way she kept glancing over at me, her brown-eyed gaze so intense I wanted to look away, but couldn't...how can I convince her to have coffee with me?

Elora Kalivas deserves a better man. So why can't I just walk away?

2

Elora

The phone blares, startling me from sleep. I barely moved after yesterday's seizure, and as I roll over and open my eyes, I wince against the light slashing through the part between the curtains. I've probably slept fifteen hours, yet I still feel groggy and muddled. A quick glance at the screen before I answer the call tells me it's well after nine, so I can't tear the caller a new one.

"Elora?"

Oh God. I recognize that voice—or at least, how he says my name. "Milos? How did you get my number?"

He doesn't speak for so long, I wonder if the call has dropped, but then he clears his throat, and his voice has lost some of yesterday's commanding tone. "When I told Elizabeth how far I'd managed to insert my foot into my mouth, she gave me your card."

My cheeks heat at the memory of my own missteps. "Well, she's probably not going to need it." I can't help the bitterness creeping into my tone. I accepted what happened. No matter how careful I am, if a seizure threatens, I'm helpless to fight it. But the shame of that night so long ago is burned into my memory, as is my father's reaction. His screams telling me how I ruined his chances of reelection, my mother's tears of embarrassment, the news stories that circulated for months... Now, living in the States, I'm spared the rumors, but five minutes with a hot Greek god and my childhood comes rushing back.

Shifting in bed, the pain in my hip reminds me before I ran out of the coffee shop, probably offending Elizabeth, I started the day by falling on my ass. Oh shit. "The boxes!"

"What boxes? And why wouldn't Elizabeth need your number? You are designing her rings, yes?"

I barely hear him as I scroll through my messages. Two from Devan, one from Mac, and two missed calls from another Boston number. I must have slept right through them. "Shit, shit, shit," I mutter. "I have to go. I owe Devan boxes to replace the ruined ones from yesterday."

"Wait. Give me five minutes. Please."

I'm tugging on pants, but something in his voice stills my frantic movements. I'm already a day late. What're five more minutes? "Okay."

"Uh," he stammers, and I think it's cute that such an imposing man is suddenly unsure. "I'm sorry for what I said yesterday. I just...I grew up hearing about you. Greece's fragile princess. Cursed to become vrykolakas. My mother talked about you for a month after the 'incident.' The papers had such outrageous claims—"

I snort, remembering how awful the rumors were and how I'd cultivated them, desperate for attention. "I was fifteen. I don't care how much makeup I wore or how often I pranked the citizens of Oia. No fifteen-year-old deserves to be called a vampire. And I'm not fragile. I had a seizure."

"I know." His voice drops, and the deep timbre calms me like a cat's purr. "You have a Wikipedia page."

"Fuck." My eyes burn as flames engulf my cheeks. Anonymous among the half a million people in Boston, I forgot what my name means back in Greece. I couldn't walk down the street in Oia without someone calling my name, asking me how many I'd cursed this week, or how it felt to be my family's greatest embarrassment. Though moving here wasn't my choice, I leapt at the chance to escape and start a new life. My mother's US citizenship helped pave the way, along with my aunt's generosity, and California became my new home. Los Angeles provided a sea of humanity, and I bobbed along on the waves, content to lose myself among starlets and valley girls, surfers and goths. For a sixteen-year-old desperate to forget her mistakes, the change felt like heaven. "Your five minutes are up, Milos. I accept your apology. Please convey my regrets to Elizabeth. I wish I could have helped her with her rings."

"Have coffee with me."

I pause, my finger hovering over the disconnect button as my embarrassment takes a backseat to desire. His tone, that deep rumble, is back, and I'm not even sure what he said, just how his voice made me feel. "What?"

"Elora, can I buy you a cup of coffee? Or hot chocolate at the ice rink? Please?" Hope colors his words, bright and bold, and I can no longer hear him breathing on the other end of the line. Why would he do this? He's read my Wikipedia page. And he's seen, firsthand, my lack of coordination and poise under pressure. "Elora?"

I don't think—that's the only explanation for my response. "When?"

"I'm not needed after three."

I can't concentrate. My gaze keeps finding the clock, but the minutes crawl by. I shouldn't be this nervous—or excited—that I can't work. Especially not since those two messages from the unknown Boston number were Elizabeth Bennett. By some small miracle, she still wants me to design her rings, and I've started and abandoned a dozen different sketches so far. None of them feel right, and I hope the appointment to see her tomorrow will provide some inspiration. Getting to know her, even a little, can only help, but I'm nervous I'll make a fool out of myself once more.

A few minutes before three, I shrug into my coat and pull a knit cap over my hair. I've done my best to cover up the dark stain smudging my cheek, jaw, and neck, and spent too long giving myself a smoky eye—two even. Working at home, I rarely take the time to put on makeup. But now, as I carefully navigate the snowy sidewalks, I feel pretty, and I vow to make an effort a bit more often.

The city sparkles this time of year, both from the lights winding around every lamppost and the snow falling gently around me. A flake lands on my nose, and I tip my head up, smiling. Snow is rare in Greece, and despite my penchant for skidding on the ice, I fall in love with this city all over again every winter.

Fifteen minutes later, the ice rink at Boston Common beckons. Milos waits along the rail, and when he sees me, his eyes light up. I smile, the flutter in my belly an unfamiliar sensation, and quicken my steps.

"I worried you would not come." He offers me his elbow, and as I wrap my hand around his arm, I catch a whiff of his after-shave. Summers along the Aegean, the salty spray, and a hint of spice.

Why does he have to smell so good?

We stop at the hot chocolate vendor, and Milos insists on paying. With steaming cups of rich drinking chocolate clutched in our gloved hands, we huddle at the viewing platform and watch the skaters spin by. Milos breaks the silence. "I shouldn't have pried."

Against the frigid winter air, my cheeks flame. I pause to sip my drink, trying to figure out what to say. He's so sincere, and I can't let him flounder in the storm I caused. "I last spoke to my family ten years ago. Everyone's happier that way. I don't embarrass them, and they don't make me feel like I'm a failure."

He doesn't respond, and I hate awkward silences, so my mouth refuses to shut up, even as my brain screams at me to change the subject. "I was born on Easter. That alone would have been enough to start the rumors. But the summer I turned thirteen, I discovered red highlights in my hair." I tick the strikes against me off on my fingers. "Gray eyes, red hair, born on a Holy Day, and cursed with this?" I pull back my hair to reveal the discolored skin along my cheek. "My father wanted to run for Speaker, and I hated him with the passion of a teenager rebelling against her parents. So I played up the part. I'd sneak out and knock on doors at night; I stained my hands red more than once. My parents forbade me from attending any political events, but that made things worse. The papers went after my father for hiding his *vrykolakas* child away from society. So he dragged me to the state dinner, even though he knew I wasn't feeling well. I had a seizure and knocked over a precious sculpture. I can't be trusted around anything delicate—or so my parents told me. A few months later, my father shipped me off to my aunt in California." I clench my teeth, the anger and hurt welling inside me as my father's words echo in my head.

Milos looks away, and the uncomfortable set of his shoulders should stop my verbal vomiting, but I can't seem to rein it in. "Aunt Olivia's funeral brought my mother to the States, but she barely said two words to me. I made sure those bridges were burned beyond repair in college."

"You've never gone home?" He peers at me, a set of lashes any woman would envy framing his eyes. Up close, his dark brown irises hold hints of golden caramel, and I want to lose myself in their depths.

"No." I can't say more. I miss Oia too much. I dream of her sparkling waters, her fresh air, and her deep cobalt skies. And the food. My God, the food. My stomach registers a vague protest even now, and the bite of rosemary, cinnamon, and nutmeg from my mother's cooking tickles my tongue.

As he rests his hand on my forearm, I allow myself one more moment to wallow. And then I shove regret, hurt, and loneliness away and force a smile. "I'm at a disadvantage. You've read my Wikipedia page. But I don't know anything about you. Well, other than your employer."

His gaze shifts to the skaters twirling around the rink, and his shoulders hunch slightly. "You remember the problems Mr. Fairhaven and Elizabeth had last year?" He takes a sip of his drink and then blows out a slow breath, the steam mixing with that from the hot chocolate.

"Yes. He got shot, right? Something about embezzlement with Elizabeth's former firm?" The whole city obsessed over Alexander's health, and then some dust-up with his brother threatened to steal the headlines, but I don't remember much about the elder Fairhaven's problems.

"Two entitled, greedy, and despicable men wanted her...out of the way. Mr. Fairhaven called my employer to request trustworthy bodyguards for her. The men who tried to hurt Elizabeth are gone now—one dead, one in jail, but they requested I stay on." Hints of sadness and anger color his words, and I search my memory for reports of the attack. I vaguely remember another man—a fellow bodyguard? —dying.

"Is she still in danger?" A pang of concern twists my stomach, quickly soothed by his assurances that he's employed only as a precaution now. He doesn't speak of the other man, and I don't want to pry into a painful memory, so I shift the subject. "What led you to become a bodyguard?"

"I come from a small neighborhood in Athens—Kallithea—and my family struggled to get by. Three sisters, a brother, my parents, grandparents, all living under one roof. The military provided me all I needed. Food, shelter, training, and a way to ease the burden on my parents. When my service ended, I tried to get a job in construction, but the economy... I was down to my last hundred euros when my former commanding officer called and offered me a job in the States. He paid well—enough for me to send money home. Mr. Fairhaven pays better. I can help my parents live comfortably now, and my sisters and brother as well."

Mesmerized by his voice and the way his lips move when he speaks, I don't notice that I'm shivering in the light flurries until Milos presses closer. When his arm drapes over my shoulders, I snuggle against his side. There's something instinctual about clinging to a larger man, and I feel safe and protected, despite barely knowing him. "Want to head somewhere warm?" I say as I peek up at him. "If you don't have to go back yet."

"I have all night." His smile alone could probably stave off the cold, but his words send a thrill racing along my spine.

Nerves flutter—though I wouldn't sleep with him on the first date. But Milos does something to my insides I can't resist. As we exit Boston Common, I wonder just how cut he is under his sweater, and fantasies take hold. Paying no attention to my steps, I stumble over an errant cobble. Milos catches me before I fall and now I know what his arms feel like around me. How much better would they feel if we were naked?

"Careful," he whispers before he dips his head and presses a hesitant kiss to my lips. I don't resist, and as he pulls away, the heat in his gaze banishes the last of the icy tingles from my toes.

We don't speak of the kiss as we wind our way through the

crowds at Quincy Market and down an alley. The flight of stairs is narrow and long, but when we emerge at the top, the secret bar I discovered four years ago beckons—three fireplaces and cozy little booths dotted along the windows that look out over the sparkling lights of downtown. We're early enough for my favorite table where I can tuck myself into a corner, warmed by the fire with the entire city spread out below me. Milos slides into the booth, looks to me with uncertainty in his gaze, and when I smile, scoots close enough for me to rest my hand on his thigh.

Once we have hot toddies and a plate of bacon-wrapped dates in front of us, he takes my hand and runs his thumb over my ring. "Your work is beautiful. You do this as a career? Or—?"

"I quit my full-time job last year to focus more on my jewelry. I have a nice contract with one of the vendors in the market, and I do well online. When I need to supplement my income, I take on some short research contracts with the Department of Urban Forestry. I studied to be a data analyst." Pride swells as I remember the day I gave my notice at the Northwest Financial Group. No one believed I could make a go of selling jewelry, but I've done pretty well. "I also spend a couple of afternoons a week doing elder care. Mostly cooking and picking up prescriptions, that sort of thing."

"Are you certain you're real?" he asks, and the awe in his voice makes me blush.

I shrug. "Spending time with the older women reminds me of my *giagiá*." I stop short of telling him the job makes me feel like I still have a family. "They treat me like a granddaughter, asking about my day, telling me stories of lost loves, offering me advice." And pat my arm as they warn me not to wait too long to marry, or quiz me about my mostly non-existent love life.

"Your *giagiá* is gone?" Milos twines our fingers, and the tender touch, along with the sympathy in his eyes, almost spurs me to be honest with him, but first dates that delve into long-held family grudges? Awkward.

"Not…exactly. But I don't speak to her anymore." I change the subject, asking him to tell me about his sisters, and he does so with gusto. They're both married now, and he has three nieces and a nephew under the age of four. "I miss them." The faraway look in his eyes matches the emptiness in my soul.

"Do you see them often?"

"No. Mr. Fairhaven is fair. Generous with vacation time. He paid for me to spend a week in Greece last fall, and when Elizabeth had her appendix out in May and recovered at home for two weeks, he helped me bring my youngest sister to Boston. Even invited her over for dinner once Elizabeth could entertain. But we are a close family, and Skype does not let me walk the vineyards with my father or help my mother with her laundry. I'm happy here—please don't misunderstand. But being half a world away is hard."

"When will you see them again?" Longing for my own family flares, deep and agonizing, but I try not to let my feelings show.

His eyes light up, and his smile dazzles in the restaurant's lights. "Three weeks. My parents, my sister Isadore, and her two daughters will spend Christmas here. Between my holiday bonus and my savings, we arranged the trip. I cannot wait to show Alesia and Dori the Boston Christmas tree. I have three full days off to spend with them."

A piece of my heart twists painfully as I think of my brother. Darian would love Boston—at least, the Darian I knew. I think of him every day, but during the holidays, my thoughts turn more often to what I've lost. He's twenty-four now. Old enough to have children of his own. Milos takes my hand, concern darkening his eyes. "Elora, did I say something wrong?"

I force a smile and wrack my brain for an acceptable response —one that doesn't turn our evening sour—until I see one of the wait staff bring over a plate of warm cookies for the table next to us. "No, not at all. Just thinking about holiday traditions. What's your favorite kind of Christmas cookie?"

Two hours later, we're stuffed full of tapas, and we've nursed our hot toddies long past the point they could even be called lukewarm. Milos insists on paying, and I reluctantly let him, then allow him to help me with my coat. I don't want this night to end, both because he's easy to look at and has the voice of an angel and because I don't think starting anything with him is a good idea. I'm not what he needs. Or he's not what I need. Every time he speaks of his parents or his sisters, his eyes soften, the love he has for his family shining through. And I'll never set foot in Greece again. My sorrow and anger at my family's betrayal threatens to overshadow this wonderful man at my side.

He asked me out because he thinks I'm someone I'm not. Or he did before my confessions tonight. I disappeared from public life, yes. But no one knew the extent of the rift that fractured my family. To most, I'm the misunderstood Greek daughter who just happens to live in Boston. But to my family, I'm the outcast—the one no one speaks of in polite company but whispers about behind closed doors. I accept my role—most of the time—and I'm happy with my life here, even if I ache for my mother's embrace, my father's approval, my brother's raucous humor.

Milos walks me to the T station, and before I disappear down the steps, he slides a hand around my back and guides me against him. His other hand brushes my hair away from my face—from the deformity I hide from the world, and I pull away so that my hair falls back over my cheek again. "Don't."

"Elora, you're beautiful. You don't have to hide from me." His words sound so sincere, and when he cups my neck, preventing me from withdrawing further, I let him. "I want to see you again." His lips find mine, and I taste the last of the whiskey, a hint of the flourless chocolate cake we shared while talking about my college roommate's hatred of all things peppermint. When his tongue traces the seam of my lips, I open to him, and as he invades the walls I've carefully crafted around my heart, I'm too slow to protest. One date and I want more. Much more. Melting in his arms, I try to commit everything about this moment to memory. The din of the crowds around us, the smell of chestnuts roasting a dozen feet away, and the feel of his fingers against my skin.

"Can I take you to dinner on Saturday?" His breathless words shouldn't fill me with sadness. I should agree, smile, and kiss him back for all I'm worth. But that wouldn't be fair to either of us. I step out of his arms, pull my coat tightly around my body, and angle my purse in front of me like a shield.

Milos, I wish I could say yes. I haven't had a night like this in ages. But I'm not who you think I am. I'm not the woman you need. I'm sorry. I've never wanted to be someone else as badly as I do right now. Those are the words running through my head. I even rehearsed them on the walk from the bar. But before I can say his name, I'm nodding, and the relief that brightens his smile banishes my fears down to the deep recesses of my heart to be saved for a time when I can't still taste him on my lips.

3

Elora

*T*he cab drops me off at the Fairhaven house at two the next day. I gawk a little on my way up the steps, the pristine white columns wrapped in garland, candles burning in every window. If the inside doesn't smell like Christmas cookies, I'll eat my hat.

Elizabeth greets me at the door, stress apparent in her tousled hair and lack of makeup. "I'm so glad you're here. Come with me." She takes my arm and pulls me through a lavish foyer and into a formal living room. Yep. Christmas cookies. Two leather sofas face one another in front of a roaring fireplace flanked by floor-to-ceiling windows that look out onto a small backyard.

Alexander Fairhaven lounges on one of the couches, a mug of coffee in his hand, crisp white shirt open at the collar. When he sees me, he uncrosses his long legs and rises. As he holds out his hand, I can't help but stare. He's every bit as handsome as he appears in the papers, but a charisma infuses his entire being that photos can't convey. "Miss Kalivas, a pleasure to meet you."

"Elora, please."

"Elizabeth showed me photos of your work, Elora. Are you certain you have the time to complete our rings before New Year's Eve?"

"Oh yes." I take a seat when he gestures to the opposite couch. "If we can settle on the basic design in the next two weeks, we'll be fine. I don't take on a lot of commissions over the holidays; you and Elizabeth will have my full attention."

Elizabeth fidgets next to him until Alexander rests his hand over hers. "Elizabeth prefers I not meddle too much in the wedding plans. Something about my tendency to choose the most lavish or expensive option..."

"We do *not* need Neil Lane designing our rings," she says with a frown. "Nor do we need Mario Batali catering the whole affair."

"Elizabeth, Mario's a friend. And you are rather fond of his lasagna." He chuckles and lifts Elizabeth's hand to his lips, brushing her knuckles with a kiss as he closes his eyes. This is love if I've ever seen it, and though I've spent exactly five minutes with them, there's no question that Alexander adores her. "I'll leave you if you don't need me."

"Go take over a small country." Elizabeth pushes him away without malice, and she grins as he stands, not letting go of her hand until the last minute.

"Oh, wait." I fumble for my bag and withdraw my sizing kit. "I need to know what size you are."

"Neil measured me as a ten."

"That may be, and I feel like an idiot for saying this, but I always do my own sizing. I have to check three different width bands. Without a finalized design, I don't know how wide your band will be, and each fit differently. Sit and relax your fingers?"

He obliges, and after a few minutes, we settle on a small range of sizes depending on what Elizabeth chooses for a design. "You're free now." I can't believe I'm teasing *Alexander Fairhaven.*

"Samuel will bring in some coffee. It was a pleasure meeting you, Elora." He heads for the hall, and I wonder how Elizabeth has gotten used to having staff. From what I've read about her, she had next to nothing when she and Alexander started dating, even though she runs a very successful accounting firm now with clients like the Red Sox. Her big score this year, the Boston Pops, made the front page of the financial section.

Once we're alone, Elizabeth skirts the table between us and takes a seat next to me. "So, what do we do next?"

Two hours and a dozen sketches later, we're making progress. Elizabeth knows exactly what she wants. The problem? She has zero idea how to describe what she sees inside her head. She's a literal, analytical woman—helpful for an accountant, not so much for design work. "Thank you," she tells me as I pack up my sketchbook and the sizing kit. "You've got the patience of a saint. I'm sorry I'm so much trouble."

"You're no trouble." I rub my temple where a headache's started to brew. "These are your wedding rings. They need to be perfect. Plus, you're paying for all of this."

She laughs and relaxes into the cushions. "You went out with Milos last night."

Oh God. Of course, she knows. She gave Milos my number. The man protects her...does he confide in her as well? "Uh, yes."

"And?" When I don't reply, she elbows me gently and lowers her voice. "He's been here for a year now. And he only stopped calling me 'Miss Elizabeth' two months ago. Did you have fun? Milos needs fun."

Heat creeps up my neck, settles in my cheeks. If my ears get any hotter, I'm going to set my hair on fire. My mouth suddenly feels like the Sahara, and I retrieve the glass of water Samuel brought for me an hour ago. The liquid slides down my throat and gives me enough time to formulate an answer. "I agreed to see him again this weekend."

"Oh, that's wonderful! I won't pry. Much. I just want to see him happy. He saved my life last year, and it cost him dearly. I worried for so long—I still do. He's more than an employee. He's a good listener and loyal to a fault. And he's lonely."

Milos

When I climb the back stairs from the downstairs staff lounge, I hear Elizabeth. "...and he's lonely."

Elora stammers an unintelligible reply. Though I can't hear her words, her tone speaks to embarrassment, and I rush up the last few steps to try to save her.

The two women turn to me, and Elora's gaze immediately drops to her boots, sending her hair tumbling over her face. In the next breath, though, she looks up at me with a small smile curving her lips, and I return the gesture. *Shit. I'm in trouble.*

The simple coral sweater sets off her olive skin. She wears very little make-up, and if we were somewhere private, I'd have her in my arms already, my hand in her hair, kissing her until she forgot her own name.

"Milos," Elizabeth says, "can you drive Elora home? I'm staying in this afternoon."

Fighting not to grin, I nod. "Of course, M—err, Elizabeth." I lose the battle and break into a full smile when I turn my gaze to Elora. "I'll pull the car around front."

"You don't have to," she protests, but there's little conviction in her words, merely a polite need not to be a bother. I know the feeling.

Elizabeth shoots me a look that plainly says *I've got this*, and I head for the garage where Mr. Fairhaven rents space for the limo, town car, and his personal vehicle, a top-of-the line Mercedes. As I turn up the heat in the town car, I start to worry. Do I offer Elora the back seat? I'd rather she sit up front. Will Elizabeth grill me when I get back? Will I get to kiss Elora again when I drop her off?

My mind is still racing when I pull in front of the house. Elizabeth embraces Elora on the front steps, and I rush over to take her arm and accept her bag. There's still too much ice on the ground.

"You're not going to make me sit in the back, are you?" she asks once I've stowed her bag in the trunk.

"No."

Say something else, you dolt.

Except, I'm frozen as I hold her door open. I haven't felt this uncomfortable and out of my element since my first girlfriend when I was fifteen. "All in?" I ask once she's settled, then shut the door after her nod. I don't know why I'm so nervous, except I don't want Elora to pity me or think I'm desperate for company and that's why I'm interested in her.

Her scent fills the car, wrapping me in a blanket of gardenias and lilacs. "Where can I take you?"

"Anywhere—" Elora's mouth opens and closes, then she tries to stifle a laugh, and it escapes as a delicate snort. "I'm sorry, my brain likes to mouth off to me sometimes. I...uh...live a block away from Artist's Grind. On Teagan Street."

I pull away from the curb, and for the next few minutes, silence fills the car. Finally, I work up the courage to glance over at her. "How did your meeting with Elizabeth go?"

Elora chuckles, and the sound diffuses all the tension

between us. "Good, I think. She's so...enthusiastic. Real, I guess. I don't know why, but I expected her to be more aloof."

"She's anything but aloof." I won't talk about my employer out of turn—I'm paid for my discretion as well as my skills, but thankfully, Elora doesn't ask me to elaborate.

Staring out the window, her heart-shaped mouth curves into a smile as we pass Boston Common all lit up for the holidays, then turn into the North End. "I love Christmas," she says. "The snow makes the city all soft and bright. Growing up where I—we —did, I thought I'd hate the cold, but every time I have to bundle up, I remember how beautiful Boston looks blanketed in white."

Giuseppe's neon sign distracts me, and my memories race to the surface.

Red blood stains the snowy sidewalk. Carl stares into nothing. A nameless man holds his belly as his life ebbs away. Mr. Fairhaven gasps for breath, and Elizabeth screams.

"Milos?" Elora slides a warm hand onto my thigh. "Are you all right?"

Wrestling for control of my emotions, I tense my fingers on the steering wheel, thankful that my gloves hide my knuckles— even with my olive skin, they'd be white by now. "Yes," I reply once I think I can do so without biting out the word. "I should have taken a different route. I don't like driving down Hanover Street."

"How come? There are some great little restaurants here." She smiles, all boundless enthusiasm. "I don't go out a lot, but when I do, I always end up in the North End."

Do I tell her? I hate lying, and all she'd have to do is Google Elizabeth and she'd learn all she needed to know. "Mr. Fairhaven was shot just off of Hanover Street. Bad memories there."

"Oh." As Elora squeezes her fingers, I risk a quick glance. Concern darkens her gaze.

At the next stoplight, I cover her hand with mine and change the subject. "Where should we go on Saturday? Do you like seafood?"

Elora

My little street didn't offer any parking when Milos dropped me off, so we settled for a quick kiss before an impatient cab driver honked at us. Now, back in my apartment, I turn Elizabeth's words over and over again in my mind.

I like Milos. Perhaps more than I've ever liked a man after a single date. Whether because of our shared heritage or simply a case of the right person at the right time, there's something about him I want in my life. But insecurities creep in. By the time I've cooked dinner, I've talked myself into a storm of self-doubt.

How can I be enough for him? Me, the outcast. Me, who'll never be "normal." Me, who might one day lose the sight in my other eye or have a seizure cause permanent damage. Who can't dance or run because my right leg will always be weaker than my left. And we won't even talk about the dark red swath of skin I hide under sweaters and scarves. The genetic lottery didn't choose me to win—unless you call Sturge-Weber syndrome luck. My parents spent a fortune on treatment, and they managed to lighten the discoloration on my cheek and jaw. But once I take off my clothes, there's no denying I'm damaged. Glaucoma took my sight in one eye, and though so far my left eye is symptom-free, I live each day with the knowledge my body might one day betray me further.

If that weren't enough, I'll never feel comfortable in Greece again. Milos is Greek to his core. Our native land weaves through his soul, and I can't return. The pain would destroy me.

I should cancel Saturday, but then I hear Elizabeth's words. *"Milos needs fun."*

I can do fun. I can't do serious, long-term relationships, but I can definitely do fun. He suggested dinner at the Salted Sea, and I know just where to go after we've plied ourselves with oysters and clams.

The week passes, and I see Elizabeth three more times, trying to get closer to the perfect design she has locked away in her head. More often than not, Milos is there, and once we go outside, our breaths escaping in puffs of steam, the cold prickling our cheeks, he kisses me until I can't remember my name. We steal moments, sharing bits of our lives, and then he drives me home, and those are my favorite times because we sit close enough for me to smell his aftershave and offer him a quick kiss at stoplights. He walks me upstairs to my apartment where I get to lean against him and enjoy the strength of his embrace and the racy suggestions he whispers in my ear.

On Friday, at my apartment door, he slides his fingers into my hair and tells me I'm beautiful. I melt, and he captures my mouth, his lips hungry. Warmth floods my core, and his need presses against my hip. Two can play at this game, and I cup his length through his pants, earning me a nip along my neck and a pinch to my peaked nipple.

"Wait until tomorrow, my little minx." He's backed me against the wall, and I can barely breathe, I'm so aroused. Clearly, two years with only my vibrator as a bedmate has left me wanton, and I'm about ready to beg him to take me right here in my hallway. But I know he's needed back at Elizabeth's, so I try to focus on the latest political controversy, or what I'm going to buy for Devan and Mac for Christmas. Anything but the sexy man in front of me looking at me like I'm candy.

Except the feel of him pressed against me makes all attempts at rational thought hopeless.

"What happens tomorrow?" I'm baiting him, I know, and when he cups the back of my neck so I can't look away, my breath catches at the intensity of his stare.

"Tomorrow, I want you screaming my name." Before I can react, he's gone, disappearing down the stairs with a last mischievous grin.

As Lettie, one of my elderly clients, sits under the hair dryer on Saturday morning, white clouds perfectly coiffed around a too-thin face, she listens to me go on about the past few days. When I tell her that Milos and I have plans tonight, she grips my hand tightly and fixes me with a hard stare. "You've never been in love, have you, sweetheart?"

"No." I've dated, but love always slipped through my fingers, though I admit I've never tried very hard to hold onto the emotion. Life is less painful alone, and when you've been rejected by the people who should love you, taking that risk feels like climbing the highest mountain in the world. No man has ever been worth the effort. Dating is fun, but love isn't worth the heartache.

"You can't go through life without love, Elora. And I don't just mean someone to keep you warm at night or scratch a particular itch." She grins, and though the action highlights all of the lines that crease her face, she's so much more beautiful when she smiles. "An electric blanket and a good vibrator will fix both of those problems."

"Lettie!" I can't believe I'm talking to her about sex toys. Or being talked to about them. This woman is like my surrogate *giagiá*. Ew.

"What? I'm old, not dead. My ticker's in tip-top shape. I can handle a little magic now and again."

Oh God. Save me.

"I've known you for two years. And in all that time, you haven't mentioned a single boy's name. You're smitten. I can tell."

Maybe.

Lettie dissolves into laughter. "Smitten. You tell that young man that if he hurts you, I'm going to beat him over the head with my walker. You hear?"

"Yes, ma'am. Now enough about my love life. How's your grandson doing?"

After I drop Lettie off at her apartment, spend an hour at the Waxing Spa getting pampered, and then stand in front of my closet for a truly ridiculous amount of time trying on outfit after outfit, I settle on a simple teal dress, black boots, and a scarf in a dozen swirling colors that warms my neck. I've curled my hair, so the brown locks fall in soft waves over the right side of my face, and choose a sparkly clip to highlight my good side. Makeup is a little hard when you can only see out of one eye, but after three tries, I'm satisfied. I feel pretty, and though I know I'm more or less pleasant to look at—as long as I cover up the patch of rougher, reddened skin with my hair—I haven't done a lot to make myself feel beautiful in the past few months. Too busy working. But this new—whatever we're calling it—reminds me how much I enjoy dressing up from time to time, and I vow to wear something other than yoga pants at least once a week.

Milos knocks on my door at six, and my breath catches in my throat as I let my gaze roam up and down his body. He's left a layer of stubble along his jaw, and his full lips curve in greeting. A black leather jacket molds to his broad shoulders, and he wears a black Henley over his jeans and boots. Sliding a hand over my hip, he slips inside the door. No words pass between us as he claims my mouth, and then I'm back against the wall, his hardness jutting against me. Desperate, arousal dampening my panties, I reach for him, but he captures my wrists in one massive hand and pins them over my head. I'm helpless under his touch, and my legs tremble as he cups my breast with his free hand.

My moan is lost to his kiss, and I push back, grinding my hips against him, begging for more. But too soon he releases me, and with a final, delicate kiss, backs away, challenge in his eyes. "Dinner? Or do I take you right here?"

"I'm not hungry." My stomach belies my words, and I cover my embarrassment with a chuckle. Milos takes my coat from the floor, a casualty of our momentary tryst, and as he bundles me up, I'm both touched and a little unsure. I've never had a man bounce so effortlessly between passion and chivalry before. His military training? His Greek heritage? He seems totally unaffected by the searing kiss we shared, but once I fasten the last button and look back at him, I see the discomfort on his face as he tries to adjust his dark jeans.

"Ready?" he asks as he offers me his arm.

"For anything." I meet his gaze, and in the dark depths of his eyes, I see only one reply.

Challenge accepted.

4

Elora

We order fresh oysters and bowls of clam chowder with warm rolls and crisp glasses of white wine. The perfect gentleman, Milos hasn't made a move to kiss me since my apartment, though his eyes smolder with heat whenever he looks at me.

"After the concert, would you like to go ice skating?"

I hate to dash the hopeful look on his face, but I have no choice. "I can't skate."

"I could help you. I only learned last year, but it's not hard once you get your balance." He takes my hand and squeezes, and a chunk of the wall I usually keep around my heart crumbles away.

"You read my Wikipedia page, didn't you?" I take a sip of wine to soothe the tightness in my throat, but as he shakes his head, I find I need another.

"I read the first paragraph in the coffee shop. But then I

decided I'd rather not know who the internet thinks you are. I want to know *you*."

Another piece falls away, exposing a part of me that can be hurt too easily. But playing things safe hasn't worked for me of late, and I take a chance, risking the pain of pity, of rejection, for this man who looks at me like I'm his whole world—at least at this moment. "I have something called Sturge-Weber syndrome. They think it's genetic, but no one knows for sure. I'm blind in my right eye, and the right side of my body is a little weaker than the left. So activities that require balance are dangerous. I fall—or stumble—a lot."

Shock plays over his features, but he doesn't release my hand. "Is it painful?"

"No. And most people don't see anything wrong when they look at me. But..." I have to continue because we're going to spend the night together, or at least I hope we will, and he deserves to know. "I told you I had a seizure when I was fifteen?"

He nods, and I think maybe he's already worked out what I'm about to say, but I have to say it anyway. "I have epilepsy."

Now he sits back, and the absence of his fingers on mine leaves my entire body cold. The last serious boyfriend who saw me have a seizure bolted a day later, though since I don't suffer from Grand Mal attacks, they aren't too terrible for bystanders. It's more the after-effects that are hard to deal with. I can't tell what he's thinking, and my heart can't take the fear that another relationship will break under the weight of something I can't control. "Milos?"

His brows furrow, and when he speaks, his voice carries the intensity of one completely focused. "What do I need to know if you have a seizure with me?"

The question gives me hope, and I rush to explain. "I can usually tell when one's threatening. Stress, illness, exhaustion make them more likely. I'll get flashes, halos really, and sometimes if I can lie down and relax when that happens, I can stave them off. But if not, one of two things usually happens. If my brain is affected, I'll feel like someone hit me over the head with a two-by-four, and I'll probably collapse if I'm not already sitting or lying down. I can usually get back up again within ten minutes, though I'll need to sleep for a few hours if I have any hope of functioning the next day. Sometimes my speech is affected, and I'll slur my words or say the wrong word completely.

"If I have a problem in another muscle group, it's usually my right leg or arm, and that's like a muscle cramp to end all muscle cramps. But I can often recover from that quicker, and sometimes I'm fully functional again in an hour, though I'll be tired until I get a good night's sleep."

He purses his lips and reaches for his wine. A stall tactic, I'm sure, but I see no pity in his eyes, only concern. "You won't hurt yourself? I don't need to call an ambulance or—"

"I've never been in danger of swallowing my tongue." At his shock, I offer him a small smile. "That's what everyone thinks of when they hear the word epilepsy. Grand Mal seizures can kill you or leave you permanently disabled. But there's no danger of that with me. Just make sure I get home safely and don't freak out if I suddenly refer to my bed as a baseball. Or a fluffernutter. Yes, both of those have happened."

Milos chuckles but quickly stops himself, guilt darkening his expression. I reach for his arm and squeeze the hard muscle. "You can laugh. Devan got to be witness to that last one. We'd known each other two months, and the seizure hit as I tried to pay for my coffee. One of the rare times I didn't get any warning. I kept telling her I needed my fluffernutter, and the poor woman took me upstairs to her apartment, wrapped me in a blanket, and made one of her staff go out for fluff so she could make me a sandwich. When I finally worked out why she kept trying to force a toasted peanut butter and marshmallow fluff sandwich into my hands, we both had a good laugh over it."

His furrowed brow tells me he has more questions, but the

waiter comes to whisk our soup bowls away, and I rush to change the subject before this whole night devolves into a discussion of my medical problems. I want to feel normal. I do, most of the time, but if we continue, I'll air all of my dirty laundry, and this relationship is too new and too precious for that. "Since I can't skate, after the concert, I'd rather go somewhere we can be alone."

The mood shifts, and Milos takes my hand, his thumb rubbing along the inside of my wrist. "Come home with me, Elora. I want you in my bed tonight."

Dark subjects long forgotten, a shiver prickles along my spine, and warmth pools in my belly.

Oh yes, most definitely.

The Boston Pops are brilliant, and Christmas carols fill my heart as Milos drives us to his apartment. He lives close to Elizabeth and Alexander, in an old building without an elevator, but with the most beautifully restored molding and Christmas lights dotting many of the street-facing windows. As much fun as I've had tonight, I thought we'd never get here...that time would slow to a crawl, and we'd be stuck listening to Christmas music forever when all I wanted to do was feel Milos's arms around me and pick up where we left off in my apartment.

"Are you sure you don't want me to bring you home?" He's concerned, and though there's no need, I feel fine, I do understand. When you find out your date has epilepsy, it's only natural that you worry when you'll have to see her collapse.

"I'm not fragile." I lean against him as he unlocks his door, and brush a quick kiss to his cheek. Stubble tickles my lips, and Milos drags me inside, fumbling for the deadbolt before he sinks his hands into my hair, sending my wool hat tumbling to the floor. When his tongue begs for mine, I yield and slide his jacket from his shoulders. We move as one, albeit with the stability of a drunk sailor, and by the time we reach his bedroom door, I'm down to my boots, bra, and panties. Milos reaches for the light, but I still his hand.

"No."

"Elora, let me see you."

"Please." I should be braver. I should be proud of my body; that's what all of the blogs say. Well, okay. That's what some of the blogs say. Others want you to be a size two with big boobs and sculpted abdominals. But no. I want to hide behind the darkness for a little longer. To distract him, I reach for his belt. Under my touch, he quivers, and as I let the leather slip through my fingers, he turns me around so my ass presses to his denim-clad erection. I push back against him, and I'm rewarded with a pinch to my nipple. The shock sends an electric charge to my core, and my knees threaten to buckle. But Milos holds me steady, and when he nibbles a path from my shoulder to my ear, I'm helpless to do more than moan.

"No lights tonight," he whispers. "But next time...I want to see you."

"Milos. I..." He presses me against the wall, and I whimper.

His warm fingers smooth my hair away from my neck. "You're beautiful, Elora. Don't hide from me."

Oh God. If he sees me...

I turn in his arms, and in the dim glow of the Christmas lights outside of his window, I meet the dark intensity of his gaze.

Milos takes my hands, then presses them to the hard bulge in his pants. We've parted just enough that my nipples tighten from the lack of his body heat and goosebumps race along my arms. "I want you, Elora. All of you." Caging my wrists, he lifts them over my head, and the motion raises my breasts so he can suck one lace-clad nipple into his mouth. My core tightens, and I arch my back to give him better access. I'm almost panting when he shifts his focus to the other breast, then slides his fingers beneath the edge of my panties.

"Now lie down," he says.

I obey, and in the glow of the Christmas lights, I admire his broad shoulders and the way his waist tapers to narrow hips. Ink swirls around his pectoral muscle, and down his right arm. If I ask, he'll turn the lights on, and I almost lose my resolve to hide my deformity. But I want this, so desperately, and so I lick my lips and think about occupying my mouth with other endeavors.

"Come closer." I want to run my fingers over his skin, trace the line of a scar on his side, and kiss my way over his chest. When his jeans hit the floor, he kneels on the bed and unzips my boots. Only my panties and his briefs separate us, his knees on either side of my hips, and I slide my hands up his thighs, hoping to remove one of those barriers.

Milos pins me with his body, lacing his fingers with mine and pressing my hands to the mattress on either side of my head. I can't move beyond helpless wriggling, and he grinds his hips into me. "What do you like, Elora?" His low murmur sends more heat flooding my core, and he slants his mouth over mine in a searing kiss before drawing back to meet my gaze. "This?" He closes his teeth over the curve of my neck, and I moan.

"Take...control. Take me," I beg, and he pushes himself up.

"Elora?"

Something inside me recognized the power of this man when we met, and now I want to feel every bit of that power. "I...like to be dominated, Milos. Can you—?"

His eyes flash, and I think he almost growls. The lace of my bra offers no protection, and as his teeth close over one tight peak, I fear I'll fly apart before he even gets my panties off.

"Do exactly what I say. Keep your arms up like that. Hold on to the headboard if you have to."

I'm soaked through now, and he releases my hands so he can

slide lower, kissing a line down my stomach until he's just above my mound. I grip the bottom of the headboard as the dark outline of his close-shorn hair bobs over me.

"These have to go," he says as he bites the edge of my panties.

Bared to him once the lace hits the floor, I squirm as he gently slips one finger inside me. When he adds a second and then sweeps his tongue over my clit, I cry out, waves of pleasure washing over me, carrying me away until there's only sound and feeling and the scent of Milos surrounding me. I come down in his arms, but he's still wearing his briefs, and I wonder why he's not making a move to enter me. "Your turn." My words scrape over my throat, and I fear I've alerted his neighbors with my cries.

"Not yet, *matia mou*." He plays with a lock of my hair. "We have all night." When we kiss again, I taste the evidence of my release on his lips. And then he's on top of me, his hands roving over my breasts, skimming down my sides. I wrap my legs around his hips, and the pressure of his cock against my swollen sex sends pleasure building again. I moan as I tug his briefs down to free his erection, and when he shifts so the silky material slides down his thighs, I wrap hesitant fingers around his length. He groans and thrusts against my hand.

"Do you have—"

"We're not there yet," he manages, and carefully withdraws so he can sink to his knees. When he wraps his hands around my calves and slides me to the edge of the bed, I hold my breath.

Can I come again so quickly? I've never—oh God. He laps at my throbbing bundle of nerves, his fingers gently parting my lower lips, and as he groans again, something primal breaks free inside of me. "Yes, Milos, more..."

His teeth scrape against me, and I float up, higher than before until he withdraws and presses gentle kisses to my inner thighs. Before I can protest, he's back again, this time with two fingers inside of me and his tongue skimming along the edges of where I desperately want him to be. The dance continues, with each turn around the floor sending me closer to release. With the music of my own cries in my ears, Milos slides his hand lower, and the hint of pressure against my ass as his finger demands entrance sends me shooting across the void, his name on my lips.

I barely register the crinkle of foil, but then he nudges my entrance, and I find him once again kneeling over me. "You are so wet, *matia mou*. Open for me." Splaying my legs, he sheaths himself slowly, letting me get used to his size. I fear he'll split me in two, but as my tremors subside, and I relax into the sensation, he slides deep, and the arousal I'd thought long sated flares up again. In what seems to be his favorite move, he pins my arms again, and I test his strength, and his patience, by pulling against his hold. The streetlights reflect the glint in his eyes, and he reaches down and pinches my nipple hard enough that I cry out. "I told you, Elora, *átakto korítsi*, you are mine tonight. Keep your hands off now. Let me take care of you."

I thrill at his words, and when he starts to move his hips, I resume my struggles. I want him to punish me, to take me so there's nothing left but pleasure, and maybe a hint of pain. But he's onto me now, and with one last thrust, he withdraws, flips me over, and jerks my hips into the air. He spears me, and when I push back against him, he slaps my ass. I try again, glancing over my shoulder to see the dark outline of his body against the glow of the Christmas lights outside his window. "More," I beg, and he spanks me again. Pressure builds, my core throbbing in time with his thrusts, and as he fills me even fuller, his grunts deepening, he wraps his fingers around my hair. His other arm holds my hip, digging into the soft flesh. Unable to move, helpless under his control, I close my eyes and let the world dissolve into pleasure.

5

Elora

*M*orning brings regrets, even though I don't think I've ever had sex quite that good before. I wake first, taking in Milos's sleeping form, and I want to reach out and trace the lines of his jaw, his cheekbone, his eyebrow. He frowns and a mournful sound escapes his lips, but once I touch his arm, he settles. I should snuggle close, let his warmth envelop me, but a crack in the drapes exposes the impending dawn, and if I don't get up and get dressed now, he'll—

"*Malakas!*" Milos growls as his eyes fly open and his confused gaze meets mine. "Elora." With a shake of his head, he pulls me close and buries his face in my hair.

For several minutes, he holds me, his heartbeat thudding against my breast. "I am sorry, *matia mou.* I didn't mean to wake you."

He's not steady, and I don't know if he'll appreciate my prying, but as far as I know, I've never woken up calling any of my lovers an asshole, and his desperate I know he wasn't talking to me. "I was already awake. But...what just happened?"

Milos tucks a lock of hair behind my ear. "Only a bad dream. Nothing serious. For most of the night, I slept very well. Especially after you woke me with your lips around my..." He chuckles and presses a kiss to the sensitive skin behind my ear. A shiver runs through me, and I let him have his secrets for now.

When he sits up to scrub his hands over his face, I turn over and draw the blankets up to my chin. I'm sure I've left half of my makeup on his pillow and if what's left doesn't make me look like a raccoon...well, perhaps a lovable Dalmatian?

"Elora, don't hide from me."

A flush creeps up the back of my neck. "I should get dressed. Can you...find my clothes?"

"It's not even six," he says. "Stay a little longer. Have coffee with me. In bed. Naked."

Not my favorite word. Naked. Naked means he'll be able to see everything. "Do you at least have a shirt?"

"Why? I know your body, *matia mou*. All the little sounds you make. How you taste. Are you afraid I won't like what I see? I'm not that shallow." The sharp edge to his voice fades as he drags his knuckle along my jaw, right over the edges of the discolored skin. "You're beautiful. Soft in the right places, strong in the others—and the trust you gave me...I'm honored. Don't hide from me now."

Milos leans down on his elbow, and despite my death grip on the sheet, manages to draw the thick cotton away. He presses a kiss to my shoulder, then skims his fingers over the darkened and reddish skin that stretches all the way to the top of my breast. "Do you think this makes you anything other than beautiful?"

"Of course it does." I bite out the words, hearing the whispers of my mother and father, my first boyfriend, the college girl who dated that same first boyfriend right after me. I don't like being so shallow, but society made me this way—society and the people who should have loved me. "You weren't supposed to see me like this."

"We spent the night together. How were you planning on keeping this from me? *Mi me empistévesai?*"

When he speaks our native language—*don't you trust me?*—something inside me melts. "I want to," I whisper. My eyes burn. I haven't cried in forever, but suddenly, the lump in my throat threatens to choke me.

"Elora, we all have scars." Milos drops his gaze to his side. "Inside and out. I can't change what I've done in my life. As much as I want to. Nor can you change how you were born."

"I know," I say quietly. "But you don't understand. Where other children played outside and ran and jumped and tumbled, I had physical therapy. My parents were devastated. The doctors told them I might be developmentally delayed, might not ever walk, might be blind by my fifth birthday. I excelled at academics. But I couldn't keep up with the other children on the playground, and they teased me for how I looked. They called me names; sometimes they'd push me. I had my first seizure in the classroom at eight. After that, my mother pulled me out of school and paid for private tutors. I had three procedures to lighten the stain on my cheek and jaw, but by then, I'd lost my sight in my right eye.

"And then they forced me to go to that state dinner." I pull out of his embrace and clutch the pillow to my chest. "If I'd told them...I knew I was at risk for a seizure. I *knew it.* But I also wanted to go, and deep down, I wanted to embarrass him, to make him pay for some stupid teenage fight I'm sure we'd had."

"Your father?" Milos doesn't try to touch me again, for which I'm thankful. This is hard enough to confess without him comforting me. And way beyond the casual bit of "fun" I'd wanted this to be. "This is why you no longer speak to them? Because of that night?"

"I embarrassed them in front of the President. And my father made no secret of his disappointment. He'd had enough of my playing the vampire. They'd indulged my geek phase, my goth phase, but the vampire ruse had to go. For a year, they kept me at home, never taking me to their public events, always making some excuse for my absence. When my aunt offered to let me live with her in California, I begged my parents to let me go. Turns out, I didn't have to. My father agreed immediately. I only found out later, he asked her to take me. I know I forced his hand. Testing boundaries, needing to see how far I could push him. I just never thought...I'd push him far enough he wouldn't love me anymore."

"I'm sure he still loves you."

Shaking my head takes too much effort, and I slump back, no longer caring about hiding. He's seen me now. More than my body, he's seen a little piece of my soul, and what he does next may inform whether we're ever naked in his bed—or any bed —again.

When he covers his hand with mine, I fear I'll break. But I hold on for dear life as he presses a kiss to my shoulder. "Parents should not abandon their children."

"Mine never got the memo."

Milos pulls me close. "Elora, I don't care about this." He smooths a hand over my stained shoulder. "Or this." Cupping the back of my head, he feathers a delicate kiss over my right eyelid. When I open my eyes, a gentle smile curves his lips. "You are beautiful and talented. You have never tried to speak to them?"

I lay my cheek against his chest and draw strength from his heartbeat under my ear. I've never confessed this truth before. Not to Devan. Not to my best friend in high school. Not to anyone. Rejection stings when it comes from friends or coworkers. But when your own family sends you away, the pain will drag you under, pull you out to sea and leave you marooned on the island of despair.

"I could have repaired the rift, I think, until college. Midway through my junior year, after one long, drunken night, I called my father and told him I hated him for sending me away. For not loving me or accepting me like a father should. This wasn't the outraged teenage hate that all children go through, but real, adult, vile and disgusting hate. I haven't spoken to him since, though I send him a card on his birthday every year."

We fall into silence, his fingers gently tracing patterns on the back of my neck. The weight of my family drama never leaves me, but my confession lightens the load, and I take a steady breath.

Four years of therapy helped me work through the pain of my family's betrayal, and I make a mental note to call for an appointment as soon as I get home to talk about all of this as the wounds bleed anew. But only a trickle, because now, there's a man. A strong, caring, patient man who wants more of me than I thought I could give. And yet I yielded to his demands, exposing the secret shame I've carried since childhood. As he rubs my back and kisses the top of my head, I wonder if I've found a man who'll accept me—scars and imperfections be damned.

Milos

As I start the coffee pot, I try to understand how her parents could treat her with such disdain. My family has always supported me. My mother hated that I joined the military, even though they needed the money. She cried for a week when I moved to the United States. Yet, she never once offered me anything but her unconditional love and support.

I'm not due at the Fairhavens' until eight, and I'd like to spend at least another hour with Elora—naked—try to take away some of the sadness she carries. But once she finished her confession, she locked herself in the bathroom saying something about raccoon eyes.

My gaze strays out the small window where light flurries swirl in the wind. So different from back home.

"That smells good." Elora interrupts my memories as she slides her arms around my waist and rests her cheek against my shoulder.

"My mother sent me an *ibrik* for Christmas last year." I turn off the stove and lift the copper pot, inhaling the slightly sweet and rich scent.

Elora leans against the counter as I fill two demitasse cups with the slightly sweetened dark brew. She's found my shirt, and the black cotton drapes over her breasts in a way that makes me never want the shirt back. Without a trace of makeup, the reddish stain on her cheek is more prominent, and she's urged her hair over the right side of her face.

Threading my fingers through her brown locks, I lift the curtain of curls and press a kiss close to her ear. "Breakfast?"

With the coffee steaming on the counter, a different type of heat springs up between us, and she slides her hands down to cup my ass through my briefs.

"If you want your coffee," I say as I grind my hips against hers, "you'll step back. Or I won't be able to resist you."

She laughs, a happy, light sound I want to hear again, then plucks her cup from the counter and saunters back to the bedroom, her hips swaying.

"Oh, you will pay for that, you little minx." After coffee, of course. I learned many years ago never to get between a woman and her caffeine.

Monday is one of those long days where my mind wanders. Elizabeth is working at Fairhaven Tower and has three client meetings set for the day. When she works privately, my days are my own, for as long as she secures the door to her suite, there is little danger. Mr. Fairhaven's brother's gambling problems have largely subsided now that he attends meetings regularly, and though Mr. Fairhaven still receives death threats on occasion, Elizabeth has, so far, been spared. Her relationship with the press helps. She's simply too nice of a person for anyone to hate.

When she consults with clients, however, I stay close. Perched on a stool at a tall desk off to the corner of the main room, I try to concentrate on my book, but my mind keeps wandering to Elora. The way she tasted the first time I kissed her, her little moans as I drove deep inside her, the fire in her eyes as she submitted to me. It's been a little over twenty-four hours since I dropped her off at her apartment, and I can't wait to see her again tomorrow.

The ringing in my earpiece startles me, and I almost fall off the stool. "Yes," I say. Only a handful of people have this number —Mr. Fairhaven, Elizabeth, Samuel, Thomas, and the head of the Mr. Fairhaven's security firm, William Northrop.

"A suspicious package was found in the lobby. Get Elizabeth out of the building in the next five minutes. The police are on their way."

Mr. Fairhaven's voice is strained, and I'm already opening her office door. "We need to leave, now. Code yellow."

Elizabeth stares at me, gaping, for exactly two seconds until she springs into action. Sweeping her purse over her shoulder, she skirts her desk, leaving her laptop, notepads, and files scattered around her.

"What is it?" she asks breathlessly as we enter the stairwell. Her shoes clack down the first set of metal steps until she stops me, pulls off her heels, and then rushes onward barefoot.

I take her arm as she stubs her toe on a bolt poking out of the floor and swears. "Suspicious package. Probably nothing, but

Thomas will pull the limo around the block. Mr. Fairhaven will be waiting for us."

"Oh." She relaxes a little then. After the marathon bombings, Boston PD takes unknown packages very seriously, but though we've done this dance before—at Copley Place close to the 4th of July—nothing's ever come of it.

Ten floors to go, and we're both breathing heavily. By the time we reach the fifth floor, others are joining us. Security must have made an announcement. "Stay close," I say sharply when we're caught in a crowd of ten others. On alert, I watch every one of the well-dressed throng. I'm paid to contemplate the worst.

As we burst out of the building, snow falls all around us, and Elizabeth uses my shoulder for balance as she slips her feet back into her heels. Jogging carefully on the slushy sidewalks, we reach the limo where Mr. Fairhaven paces. Sirens wail on the main street, and Mr. Fairhaven bundles Elizabeth into the car. I rap on the front passenger window, and Thomas peels out.

The town car is in the underground garage, and Elizabeth will want her things if the package turns out to be nothing. So for now, I trudge back to the building, settling myself across the street until the police finish. I hope to all that's holy that this is a false alarm.

Two hours later, I knock on the door jamb of the upstairs study at the Fairhaven home. Elizabeth sits on the floor, travel brochures spread out around her. "I have your things," I say when she glances up. Stress tightens her lips, but she smiles when she sees me.

"Oh thank goodness." She jumps up and accepts her brief-case. "Alexander said it was a mix-up?"

"Of sorts. The rumor is that a stockbroker was fired from the thirteenth floor, and he boxed up several pieces of electronic equipment along with some powdered creamer from the office coffee station, then left the box in the lobby on his way out of the building." I try not to roll my eyes. By the time the box's contents were identified, the entire building had been evacuated. "The police have the man's name. He'll likely be arrested."

As Elizabeth sets up her laptop at the desk, she cocks her head and studies me. "You look tired."

"I'm fine, miss." Elora and I stayed up late texting the night before, and exhaustion presses down on me, but a brief memory flashes, and my lips twitch before I get them under control.

Elizabeth skirts the desk and approaches. "Fine? That looks like more than fine."

I meet her gaze, trying not to give anything away, and light dances in her eyes.

"I won't pry, Milos," she says with a chuckle as she touches my arm briefly. "I just want to know that you're happy."

This time, I don't fight my smile. "I am." As I turn to go, I add, "Thank you for insisting that I call her."

"You're welcome."

Elora

Elizabeth and Alexander's wedding looms—at least in Elizabeth's mind. Three voicemails and four emails in the past twenty-four hours. I've been working on her sketches, and with a dozen new ideas tucked into my bag, I ring the bell of the Fairhaven house. Samuel, the house manager, answers the door and welcomes me inside. "Miss Elizabeth is in the upstairs study. I'll take you, Miss Kalivas."

"Elora, please."

Samuel winks at me. "If you can ease her stress a bit, I'll consider your request."

I like him, and he always remembers how I take my coffee. But, there's an affection to how he treats both Elizabeth and Alexander that surprises me. Though I don't know anything about what the relationship between a billionaire and his staff should be, I always imagined things would be stiff and professional.

Samuel clears his throat at the entrance to the study. "Miss Elizabeth, Miss Kalivas is here."

Elizabeth stands at the windows, staring out over the snow-kissed streets. When she turns, I hide my reaction. She's been crying. Red patches dot her cheeks, her swollen eyelids bear no trace of makeup, and her shoulders slump. She smiles, but I'm pretty sure she's trying not to break down again.

Before she can speak, Samuel's in front of her and whispers something to her I can't make out. She nods and pats his arm. "Thank you. But there's nothing you can do. Some relationships can't be mended."

"Are you certain?"

"Yes."

He leaves silently, and Elizabeth and I sit, sinking into cushions so soft we might as well be lounging on clouds. I want to ask what's wrong, but though I suspect we might be edging towards friendship, a crying woman two weeks before her wedding is BFF territory, for sure. Instead, I pull out my sketchbook. "Let me know what you think of these. I did some research and found photos of similar rings from England in the 1820s. If your grandmother's ring was passed down, the design was probably based on the style at the time. This one," I flip open to the third design, the one I'm most proud of, "would be two-tone yellow and white gold, with the yellow gold peeking out from behind the whorls here, and optionally studded with small diamonds."

"Oh my God." She grabs the sketchbook and runs her fingers over the design. "This is perfect." Her eyes brim with unshed tears. I've hit a chord somehow, and I don't understand why. "And Alexander's ring?"

"Here." I flip the page, and she loses her battle with her emotions, dissolving into hiccupping sobs as she clutches the book to her chest. Now I don't have a choice. You don't ignore a woman's tears. You put your arms around her and let her cry. She hugs me tightly, and with the book crushed between us, I rub her back until she calms and pulls away.

"I'm sorry, Elora. I just...it's been a bad couple of days. My mother sent me a certified letter decrying my wedding and telling me how horrible I am, and I miss my grandmother so much."

The emotions tear at me, especially after my last date with Milos. "I miss mine as well," I confess, finding the words easier now that I've told him my secret. "My parents and I don't speak, and my grandmother lives with them. I send her cards on her birthday. I like to think she receives them, but I don't honestly know."

"I lost my grandmother when I was ten." Elizabeth relinquishes my sketchbook and twists the fat diamond around her finger. "When I got engaged the first time—back in Seattle—my mother offered me Grandmother's wedding band. I accepted, but she never actually let me take possession of the ring. Every time I asked, she brushed me off, claiming that she was too busy to go to the safe deposit box and get it. 'You have time, Lizzie. You haven't even picked a date yet.' The ring couldn't have been worth more than a few hundred dollars. No stone, just white and yellow gold—almost exactly like your sketch.

"My ex-fiancé..." She stops, looks down at her hands, and lowers her voice. "He treated me like a possession. A trophy. He and my mother both. I had to dress how he wanted, eat what he wanted, *be* who he wanted. When my parents disowned me, I lost him as well—and any hope of seeing the ring again."

I hesitate to ask, but we're sharing things now—or she is—and this is part of the code. "If he abused you..."

"Oh, I'm not upset that he dumped me. I was at the time because I didn't know any better. I thought he loved me, but really, he only loved the idea of me. Once he realized I wasn't going to be the perfect wife, the wealthy heir to my parents' fortune, the size four, always made-up, obedient wife, he didn't want me. But losing my parents—or finding out they cared more for appearances than for their daughter—that broke me. I spent years building myself back up, finding out who I was. Me, the real Elizabeth, not their Lizzie. I'm happy now. Believe it or not." She swipes an errant tear from her cheek. "But getting married without my family and without my grandmother, who loved me completely..."

Understanding lifts the haze, and I nod as I squeeze her fingers. "Your grandmother is always with you, Elizabeth. I can't offer you comforting words about your parents. Years of distance and expensive therapy haven't given me any answers there. Parents are supposed to love their children unconditionally. Not send them away because they're an embarrassment or disown them over business. I'm sorry they won't be here for your wedding—only because you want them to be. But from the little you've shared, I'm also glad, because they don't sound like very nice people."

Elizabeth doesn't speak for several breaths, and I fear I've been a little too open, too forward. But as I'm biting the inside of my cheek and wracking my brain for something else to say, some way to take everything back and return the discussion to her rings or the weather, she bursts into laughter. "Oh God. I really like you, Elora. You're right. They aren't nice, and they'd just ruin the wedding if they tried to come. Thank you."

I don't know what to say to that, so I pick up my sketchbook. "I have a few other designs too if you want to see them."

"No." An emphatic shake of her head reinforces the finality of the word. "Those are perfect. More than perfect, even. What do we do next?"

"I'll have wax molds for you and Alexander to try on in a couple of days, and if those fit and you're satisfied, I can have the rings finished just after Christmas."

When Elizabeth throws her arms around me, I have to brace myself so we don't tumble into the cushions. "I can't tell you the weight you've just taken off my shoulders." She gives me one last squeeze and pulls away. "I want to ask you something, and if it's too forward, just ignore me. But...will you come to the wedding?"

I don't know what to say. We've blown right past the edge of friendship with our shared confessions. I like this woman— genuinely like her—but she's soon to be the wife of the most powerful man in Boston, and this isn't my world. I design jewelry I sell in coffee shops and co-ops. She knows Neil Lane and Mario Batali. Still, the light in her eyes and the hopeful smile on her face leave me no choice.

"I'd be honored."

6

Milos

 'd like to skip this day. Just hide in bed and pretend the nineteenth of December doesn't exist. Waking up with the smell of gunpowder in my nose and my voice hoarse from screaming in my nightmares doesn't help my mood—neither does knowing I can't see Elora today. Mr. Fairhaven and Elizabeth have a business dinner tonight, though Elizabeth doesn't want to go. I'm needed until well after midnight. As I approach the house on foot, my boots crunching over the snow, I pull out my phone and text Elora.

I have tomorrow off. Can I take you to dinner?

I'll have to turn my phone off soon—I can't be distracted guarding Elizabeth, and she's going back to the office today for the client meetings she couldn't finish up the other day due to the bomb scare. Thankfully, Elora rises as early as I do and responds before I reach the back steps of the Fairhaven house.

I have to go Christmas shopping tomorrow. Want to join me? Then takeout at my place?

With a smile, I send one last message: *I'll take you at your place. Will you consider...letting me tie you up?*

Holding my breath, I wait for her reply with my hand on the doorknob. Even with the weight of the day and the nightmares that woke me repeatedly last night, I feel like I could fly when she answers.

I'll be disappointed if you don't. XOXO

This woman might be it for me. As I greet Samuel and Thomas, who gather in the staff lounge with mugs of coffee, I have to fight my smile.

"Things are going well with Elora, then," Thomas says as he sinks into a chair.

"You could say that." I pour myself a cup of the dark brew, the sight of her drinking coffee in my bed, my shirt riding up her hips and exposing peaked nipples distracting me long enough that I slosh liquid over the rim. "What about you and Mattie? How are the wedding plans coming?"

Thomas grimaces. "I don't understand why we can't just elope. But at least we have until June—that's when she finishes teaching for the year. Mr. Fairhaven approved the time off."

The morning news headlines stream over the local NPR station, and the date has a sobering effect on the all of us. We raise our mugs. "To Carl," I say.

"To Carl," Samuel and Thomas echo.

Mr. Fairhaven canceled dinner at Elizabeth's request, so a little after 7:00 p.m., I push through the door of the Greek Orthodox Cathedral. This close to Christmas, the choir sings every night, and more than once this month, I've found myself here after work, though I've never been brave enough to do more than sit in the back and listen to the music.

By some miracle, there's no line for the confessional, and I sit, head bowed, with a priest no older than I am. As he blesses me and directs my focus to the small statue of Jesus in front of me, fear overwhelms me, and my hands start to sweat. Rubbing them on my pants does little good, but the priest leans forward, his kind eyes full of understanding. "Has it been a while?"

"Many years. Too long." I should have gone the day it happened. The next and the next and the next. "I killed a man, Father. Someone who had just murdered a friend, shot my employer, and would have kidnapped and killed the woman I was protecting. I did my job. Saved two lives. But this darkness I live with now...I can't escape it."

The priest rests his hand on my arm. "The Bible says that murder is a sin. But protecting others is our duty. Was there another way you could have stopped this man?"

I shake my head to try to clear the memories, but it's no use. They're with me every day. "No, Father. He was about to kill my employer's girlfriend. The woman I was hired to protect. My partner was already dead. If I'd hesitated, Elizabeth and I would probably both be dead."

"Have you tried to atone for your actions?"

His words are kind, but I feel so guilty, I can scarcely speak over the lump in my throat. "When I served in the Special Forces, many men fell from our raids. Those men I could atone for by helping their countrymen. Their families. This man...the police never even discovered his name. I don't know how to atone for this."

The priest inclines his head. "We are taught to love all of God's people. To preserve life. To protect others. Would it have been better, kinder, to wound only? To find another way? Of course. The Church teaches that killing is wrong—even killing done in defense of others. But God sees you. He sees your pain, and He will forgive you if you ask."

As the first tear falls, the priest takes my hand, and we pray.

I couldn't settle after my confession, and I've walked for two hours, trying to find a way out of the darkness of this day. Now, I'm staring up at Elora's apartment building. We weren't supposed to see one another today, but I need her—need her to know the truth before this goes any farther.

She answers the door wearing an old, long-sleeved waffle shirt and fleece pants. Her feet are bare, her hair piled into a messy bun. "Milos?"

"I'm sorry. I should have called—"

When she pulls me into her embrace, I inhale her scent, and some of the darkness fades. "What's wrong?" Her lips brush my ear, and I sigh, needing to delay my admission for another minute or two so I can hold on to this angel in front of me.

As Elora leads me down her short hall, the scent of Christmas cookies comforts me. "Sit," she says as she points to her couch. "I'll be right back." A plate of cookies and a glass of wine rest on her coffee table, and she heads for the kitchen, returning a minute later with another glass for me.

Once she's curled at my side, I take a long sip of the rich Malbec. "A year ago—today—a paid assassin tried to kill Elizabeth. Mr. Fairhaven was shot trying to save her. There were two of us on guard duty that night. Carl...we'd worked together for a year on various projects. We were close. I'd met his family. He had a younger brother who idolized him."

My eyes burn as I find myself back in that alley. "I was outside, while Carl took a position inside the restaurant. He radioed me." Elora twines her fingers with mine as I sink into the memories.

"Code red. Rear of the building."

With my hand on my gun, I glance up and down the street. To the north, a line forms out the door of a local bakery. South. Fewer people. Easier getaway. I race for the alley, my boots skidding on the piles of snow that cover the sidewalk. The shot echoes in my ears. By the time I turn the corner, a second shot has me diving behind a dumpster as Mr. Fairhaven, fifty feet away, falls to his knees. I spare him only a glance—his orders have always been clear: protect Elizabeth at all costs—but the blood...so much of it.

She's struggling, tears streaming down her cheeks as the hitman drags her back. I raise my gun, but I don't have a shot. Not with that asshole using her as a human shield.

"Elizabeth."

Mr. Fairhaven's cry sets something loose inside her, and she screams as she wrenches her arm free, then goes on the offensive. Once she's broken the hitman's nose, she falls, and I don't think. He raises his gun at her, and I fire.

"Milos."

Clenching my hands, I fight my way free of the memories and back next to the woman I'm pretty sure I'm falling for. Elora cups my cheek. "You killed the assassin?"

Nodding, I try to avert my gaze. "You deserve...better than a killer."

"You're *not* a killer. You're a bodyguard. Did you really think I wouldn't want to be with you because you did your job? If you hadn't...Elizabeth would have died. Maybe Alexander too. And we would never have met." She's so earnest, so without guile or judgment that I don't know how to respond. Yet, something lingers in her eyes. Sadness, perhaps. "You're a good man, Milos."

"I don't feel like one today."

She leans in, and as she brushes her lips to mine, she whispers, "That's *why* you're a good man."

Under the well-worn fabric of her shirt, her nipples tighten. I trail my fingers up her hip, finding smooth skin, and she shudders as she straddles me. "Put your arms around my neck," I say as I hook my hands under her thighs. "I need you, Elora."

"Take me." Her fingers slide into my hair, and her eyes darken as I stand with her. "First door on the right."

I can already smell her arousal. Balancing on a knife's edge between control and chaos, I tighten my hold. "Do you trust me, *matia mou*? I'm not sure I can be gentle right now."

Setting her down, I struggle not to groan as she strips off her shirt to reveal her perfect breasts, the flush of excitement spreading over her skin. "Open the nightstand drawer," Elora says as she shimmies out of her baggy pants with a mischievous grin. "I went shopping today."

"I thought we were doing that tomorr—" My words die as I see the pair of black, padded handcuffs. "You..."

She holds out her wrists, a motion that offers her breasts to me like a banquet. I can't get out of my clothes fast enough, and my cock strains against my briefs as I kneel over her. Though I ache to restrain her, to make her mine in every way, my need for control—especially today—scares me. "Not yet. Lie back."

The bedside lamp casts shadows across her face as she stretches out on the bed, her curls fanning out around her face as she loosens the clip that holds her hair. I want to sink my fingers into those locks, to feel their silk slide over the backs of my hands as I claim her mouth, but I'm awestruck by her beauty, by the trust she gives me when there's so much darkness I don't know how to keep from those I love inside me.

But my confession tonight eased enough that I won't break, won't let the terrible memories consume me, and I lower myself down next to her, tracing her jaw with a knuckle. Her eyelids flutter as I lean over and take one of her dark nipples between my lips. My other hand finds the lace of her black panties, and she shudders when I brush the curls that guard her sex.

"Milos," she breathes as her legs start to shift, her heels struggling to find purchase against the sheets.

"Be still, little minx." I bite down on her nipple, just enough to send a little shock of pain racing through her body. Glancing up at her face, I grin as her eyes unfocus, and she jerks her hips. Her lips curve, the pleasure giving her a dazed, dreamy grin. "I want you begging."

Despite my earlier fears, I am gentle with her. Nibbling on her ear, down the curve of her neck, all while playing with her breasts, lightly pinching, trailing my fingers down her side to the point she giggles. Once I reach her panties again, I tug the lace from her hips, down her legs, and caress each foot. I'd love to bind her legs wide, but she only bought handcuffs from what I can see.

Scanning the room, I see her robe hanging on a hook in her closet. Elora's gaze follows me as I rise, slip the belt from the loops, and then look around for something else I can use. "Scarf?" I ask.

"Top drawer." She points to the dresser, her hand trembling slightly. "There's a ratty old green one in there."

Perfect. Once I have what I need, I kneel at the foot of her bed. "I want to tie you up, *matia mou*. May I?"

Her nod and the little catch of her breath in her throat make my cock so hard I fear I'll come just from touching her, but I force a breath out through my teeth as I tie first one delicate ankle, then the other to the legs of her bed frame. Her glistening sex beckons, but I'm not done torturing my Greek princess yet.

"I'm...I've never felt this way," she says, her voice somewhere between a whimper and a cry as I buckle one of the padded cuffs around her left wrist. "I need you, Milos. Please hurry."

When I've locked her wrists together, I gently raise her arms and guide her fingers around one of the wrought iron whorls in her headboard. "I love this bed," I say with a grin. "Perfect for any number of activities."

She writhes as I crush my lips to hers, moaning into our kiss. Her breasts press against my chest, and gooseflesh covers her bare skin. Almost gasping, she meets my gaze as I break the kiss, and the raw need in her eyes sends me scrambling lower so I can taste her.

With her legs spread, Elora's scent washes over me, her sweet, salty arousal like the finest wine as I swipe my tongue over her slick folds. She cries out, and I grab her hips, keeping her still so I can lose myself in her taste.

"Hold. On." I switch my focus to her inner thighs. "I...want... this...to...last," I say, punctuating each word with a nip or a kiss.

"I can't. Please. I need to—" Elora's whimpers take on a higher pitch, and even the bindings and my strong hands can't keep her still.

Sliding two fingers deep inside her slick channel, I trace patterns on her sensitive bud with my tongue, and with one last cry, she implodes, her entire body stilling for a single second before waves of pleasure send her muscles trembling, her cries guttural, and her release flooding over my hand, my lips, my tongue.

I take her all in, relishing her taste, but above all, her trust. Tugging lightly, I release her legs and arms, then gather her against me. My briefs dampen as a drop of pre-cum escapes my cock, but she's too far gone for me to take her yet. So instead, I hold her close, stroking her hair, until she searches out my lips and then, fuck, I can't hold back.

"On top of me," I growl as I release her, then tug off my briefs. Once I'm sheathed, she throws one leg over me, then sinks down with agonizing slowness, breathing out in a steady breath to accommodate my girth.

Elora bows her head, letting her hair hide her face, the stain on her neck and shoulder, but I reach up and brush the curls away. "No. I want to see you. All of you."

Heat blooms on her cheeks, but she tucks her hair behind her ear, and when she meets my gaze, there's no sadness, only awe. What? That I could find her attractive? "There is no woman in the world more beautiful than you are at this moment, *glykia mou.*"

We find our rhythm, her hands on my chest, my fingers digging into her ass. I strain against my need for release, needing to prolong this moment, this connection between us, but when she starts angling her hips to send her clit scraping against the wiry curls above my cock, I give up the battle. She's so close, I can send her over the edge with ease, and I reach down and swipe my finger through the arousal that coats her thighs.

"You are mine, Elora. And I am yours," I say as I press my slick finger against the rosebud of her ass, and when I breach her, we both fly over the precipice together.

7

Elora

*E*lizabeth needed Milos first thing in the morning, and so he left my bed before I'd even fully opened my eyes, pressing a kiss to my lips and telling me to lock the door after him.

In the morning light, the memories of his confession, of my wanton and desperate need to soothe something inside him and claim a bit of happiness for myself, leave me unsure of where we're going. Milos looks at me like I'm everything he could possibly want, and I feel the same way about him. Until I glance at the photo of my *giagiá* on my desk and a hole opens up inside me—one no one but my family can fill.

I spent the morning finalizing the wax sample rings for Elizabeth and Alexander, and now, I sit in their formal parlor as Elizabeth stares with awe at the beige approximation of her wedding band on her finger. "This is perfect, Elora."

"I agree," Alexander says as he slips his own wax ring off and places it gently back in the box. "I can have the diamonds for Elizabeth's ring sent to you tomorrow if you'd like."

"Great. I should be home all day." Though the diamonds for Alexander's ring came last week, Elizabeth's were larger—the only concession Alexander asked for. Milos is picking his family up from the airport late tonight, and a pang of something—longing, perhaps—stabs my heart. "I'll have the final rings for you on the twenty-seventh."

Once I've packed up my kit, Elizabeth gestures towards the kitchen. "Milos is downstairs. I'll take you."

His face lights up as he sees me, and Elizabeth gives me a quick hug before we head out the back door. "He's been grinning almost all day," she whispers in my ear. "It's so good to see him happy. And you, too."

Despite her words, I can't fight my sadness as Milos walks with me through Copley Square an hour later. I need to pick up a few gifts for Devan and Mac, and he claims to have his own shopping to do, but I think he just wants to spend time with me.

Though our lovemaking last night left me sated, exhausted, and probably in love, deep down, I want to be alone. His presence, my intense desire to let myself fall in love with this man at my side, is a reminder of all I've lost, and though I take comfort from his hand on mine, I can't help my memories from wrapping a vise grip around my heart.

When Milos starts to tell me about his family dinners growing up, and how excited he is that his parents, his sister, and two nieces will arrive late tonight, I lose the tenuous control on my emotions I've imposed over the past few days. A single tear tumbles down my cheek, and Milos stops and pulls me out of the fracas of shoppers all around us.

"Elora, what's wrong?" His strong fingers tip my chin, and I can't look away. I dream about his eyes. I see them whenever I close my own, feel his lips against my breast when I'm lying in bed at night, and imagine his talented fingers whenever my mind wanders during the day.

"I miss my family."

When he wraps me in his arms and presses my cheek to his chest, I try to draw in his strength.

"Why not call them? Perhaps your parents miss you just as much but do not know how to reach out. What harm will a phone call do?"

He doesn't understand. I tried years ago. As college graduation loomed, and I found out I'd be receiving an award, I called my father. But he refused to come to the phone to hear my apology, and the overwhelming pain of his rejection sent me to bed for a week. Between the depression and the constant threat of seizures, I barely managed to walk the stage at the ceremony. I can't risk that rejection again. I'm stronger now; therapy helped me deal with my anger and hurt, but that doesn't mean I want to risk my heart just because it's Christmas.

I don't answer, and he draws back. "Elora, my mother cooks for an army. I know we are new, but spend Christmas with us. Meet my family. I promise they won't marry us off if you join us for dinner. At least then, you won't be alone."

Too soon! Panic tightens my throat. This is why I didn't want to get involved with anyone. Especially not right before Christmas. If you're dating on Christmas, you're serious. You're in a *relationship*. I haven't done relationships in so long, I'm pretty sure I've forgotten how. And a Greek family? On Christmas? I'm more resilient now, yes, but not that strong. "I...uh...no. I can't."

Tiny lines around his lips tighten, and he looks away. "I'm sorry. I didn't mean to make you uncomfortable. Forget I asked." As he heads into a coffee shop to buy us peppermint mochas, I kick myself for overreacting and hurting this wonderful, patient man, one I fear I just might love.

We spend the late afternoon watching *White Christmas*—or trying to. He won't stop touching me, and he's teased me into three gentle climaxes, soothing me with deep kisses, his voice in my ear, calling me a treasure, his dear heart, his beautiful angel. All in Greek, of course. I yearn for more, and he keeps promising that we'll get there, though I can plainly see his cock straining against his jeans.

At seven, he runs down the street for Chinese food while I take a shower. The warm water relaxes the last remaining knots in my shoulders, but my over-sensitized nipples tighten against the spray. I ache but in the best possible way. Yet, I don't know what we're doing here. Christmas, New Year's, Valentine's Day... those are the Hallmark holidays of a relationship. A serious relationship. I wish I could make him understand I'm not who he needs, but every time my thoughts wander to that unpleasant subject, the coin flips—he may be exactly who *I* need. Then I panic, fleeing into the thrills of the amazing sex and the comfort of his understated sense of humor.

The front door clicks shut as I pull my favorite sweatshirt from the drawer: old, worn-out, with the College of the Redwoods logo finally fading away. He had some very specific requests for me when he left. No bra, no panties, no makeup, and my hair pulled away from my face. I want to hide, even though he's seen me naked more than once now, but he elicited my promise with a searing kiss, and now, as I stand in front of my bedroom mirror, I peer at my unadorned skin.

No compliment is going to stop me trying to hide the stain on my cheek and jaw, or make me give up my collection of scarves, but this is who I am, and he accepts me, so I try to accept myself.

I jump as Milos presses against my back. He approached on

my right side, and I couldn't see him coming. "Shhh, *glykia mou.*" Sweetheart. The Greek phrase melts my heart, and I relax against him as foil rustles.

With a strong hand, he bends me over my dresser. Somehow, in the minute he's been back, he's shed his clothing. He wraps his fingers around my braid, holding me still as he slides into me. I'm pinned, and with the mirror in front of me, I can do nothing but watch as he thrusts, gently at first, then at my wriggling, harder. His emotions infuse every movement, equal parts passion and... something I fear might be love. Above all, though, I see how beautiful he thinks I am. My hips are too big, my stomach hasn't been flat in a decade, but Milos worships me, and when he slaps my ass hard enough to sting, I can't stifle my whimper.

"Do you like this?" He runs his hand down my back, and suddenly his finger slides between my ass cheeks, and the subtle pressure after he's kept me floating from orgasm to orgasm all evening sends me shooting over the edge.

"Look at me, Elora." His sharp words force me to obey, and I watch myself come, watch him watch me, and when he loses his own battle against his climax, his eyelids flutter and he shouts my name.

When we've both dressed again—no, he didn't relent on the no bra or panties rule—and we're sitting on my living room floor with boxes of almond chicken and honey walnut shrimp between us, he pauses as he hands me chopsticks. "Elizabeth told me she invited you to the wedding."

I nod. Where's this going?

"Mr. Fairhaven has hired a small army of private security for the event. Once Elizabeth arrives at the hotel to dress, I'm no longer needed. Thomas, Donatella, Samuel and I are guests."

Milos is actively squirming now, so either he really has to pee, or he's trying to work out how to ask me to be his date for the wedding. I chuckle and spare him from this torture. "Do you want to go together?"

"Yes. Please." He pulls me into his lap, then tightens his fingers in my hair. "I would very much like to start the new year with you."

Despite my reservations, and another one of those holidays that signify a serious relationship looming—one with a wedding, no less—his relief infuses the room with a sense of calm. One I've been desperate for all day. I'm falling for this man, and though I fear for my heart, I wonder if it's time for me to take a risk and let myself love him.

After Milos leaves for the airport to gather his family, I work for a few hours. Well after midnight, I lock up Elizabeth's ring. I never leave anything out, just in case of a break-in, and Elizabeth and Alexander's rings are special. All the stories Elizabeth told me about her grandmother made them so. I've set the five diamonds in his ring already, and this is my finest work. Tomorrow, I'll set the diamonds in Elizabeth's ring, we'll do the final fitting on the twenty-sixth, and then they'll be done. We're cutting things close, but she's so happy with the design that I'll stay up all night, every night, until I'm done just to ensure everything's perfect.

Christmas lights twinkle on my tree, and three small packages rest underneath. Two of the gifts are from my college roommate, Morgan. The third isn't *from* anyone.

I found a used bookstore in the North End last week. I love old bookstores. The smell. The musty, crinkling paper, the scent of old glue, worn leather covers. I can spend hours just touching the spines, flipping through pages. Buried on a shelf far in the back, a book of Greek poems from Alexandros Soutsos, untranslated, possibly from the original printing in the early 1900s caught my eye. Milos has a line from one of Soutsos's poems tattooed on his ribcage.

After our...well, not a fight, but our difference of opinion earlier in the day over meeting his family, I wasn't sure I wanted to give him a gift. Would it be too forward? Too much of a mixed message? But after dinner, when we opened our fortune cookies, added "in bed" to the awkward phrases, and then lost ourselves in one another yet again, I changed my mind. I bought this for him. I'll deliver the book tomorrow and meet his family. I won't stay long, though he begged me to join them for dinner. That's too much. Too soon. But I can see him, feel his arms around me, and maybe spend a few minutes not caring that I'm going to be alone again on what had always been my very favorite holiday growing up.

Now, I stare at my phone, knowing what I'm doing is a bad idea, but unsure I can stop myself. I miss my family. My anger, fear, and longing leave me shaking, and I have to dial three times before the call connects. With the time difference, it's barely seven in the morning in Oia, but my grandmother's voice carries laughter over the line. "*Kalá Christoúgenna,*" she says. "Hello?"

"*Giagiá?*"

"What are you doing calling here?" The laughter disappears, replaced by quiet kindness that brings tears to my eyes. The back of my neck prickles with shame, and I sink down onto my couch, fighting the tears that threaten. "Your father will not be pleased." I almost hang up, but then she lowers her voice. "But I am. I have missed you, Elora. You wait. I need to go back to my room, and I do not move so fast anymore."

I sit quietly, twisting the blanket between my fingers and waiting. A door shuts, and my grandmother groans as she sits—at least that's what I imagine she's doing. "*Giagiá?* Are you all right?"

"For a ninety-two-year-old woman, *paidi mou*, I am very well. But I have arthritis, I can no longer see to read, and I broke my hip two years ago."

I hate that my parents sent me away. That I let my hatred and grief ruin any chance of rebuilding the relationship. That I haven't seen my brother in a decade, that my *giagiá* has aged so terribly since I've been gone, and that I haven't known my mother's embrace since the day I left for the United States. But right now, I put aside all my pain so I can hear my *giagiá's* voice.

We talk for half an hour, and I tell her about my life here, my work, how I see her face whenever I take care of Lettie for the afternoon.

"Is there anyone special in your life, Elora?"

I want to say no. But that would be a lie. Milos is special. Perhaps more special than I've been willing to admit. "I met someone from home. I like him, *Giagiá*. He is from Athens, and now he works for a very rich man in Boston."

"Does he treat you like a princess? Every woman deserves to be treated like a princess. If he does not, he is no good for you." Her voice sharpens. If you've never had a Greek *giagiá* upset with you, you're luckier than I am.

"He does."

"I only had twenty-two years with your grandfather. Cancer is a terrible disease. But for every one of those years, he always put me first."

I have so many questions, but none more important than the one I ask next. "*Giagiá*, can I come home? Just for a visit. I...miss Mama and Papa. I haven't seen Darian since he was twelve. I want to be a part of the family again."

"Oh, Elora." She clucks her tongue, and I can see her shaking her head as she mutters in Greek. The words fill me with despair, for she wonders aloud what she did to deserve this burden. "Darian has a daughter now. Four years old. He married a nice local girl who cooks terribly, but loves him with her whole heart. You would like her, I think, and their little girl."

"But Papa? Can I talk to him?" Fear tightens my stomach, sweat breaking out on my palms, but I have to know.

If there's even a chance.

Disappointment washes over me as she sighs. "My son is stubborn. He still refuses to even speak of you. Apollonia would take your call, I think, and I will tell her to phone you when your father leaves for work after the holidays. But Galan is too stubborn for his own good. I fear he will never come around, and I do not want to see you hurt again."

Her wish falls on deaf ears as pain radiates out from a point at the back of my skull. A halo of light obscures the Christmas tree, and I know what's about to happen. The seizure barrels closer, and I just barely manage to tell her that I love her and say goodbye before the phone slips from my hand, and I collapse against the cushions, sobbing as I writhe in agony.

8

Elora

I probably shouldn't try to navigate the T on Vicodin, but last night's seizure left me with a headache that rivals being hit with a meat cleaver. Actually, the meat cleaver probably would have been less painful.

With Milos's present tucked in my bag, I squeeze onto the Green Line and try not to fall as all of the seats are taken. The only vacant spot to stand is too far from anything to hold on to. Scanning the riders, I hope someone will offer me a seat, but they're all off in their own little worlds—like most subway patrons—and I say a little prayer the ride will be smooth.

The train jerks to a stop, and I fall against the man next to me. He's surprisingly chivalrous, steadying me with a strong hand, smiling. He shifts so I can grip the pole. "Hang on," he says. "It's too close to Christmas to end up trampled."

When I stagger off the train at the Washington Street station, the enormity of what I'm about to do almost sends me fleeing for the train again. I could ride all the way to the end of the line and get lost instead of meeting Milos's family. We've been together a little over three weeks, and while I care deeply for him, and I fear I just might lose my heart—if I haven't lost it already—are we really so "official" that I have to meet his mother, father, sister, and two nieces? And where the hell are they staying? Milos only has two bedrooms. Two tiny bedrooms. I know, as we've fooled around in both of them.

But the joy that lit up his face when I agreed to come outweighs my fears. Laughter spills through the door, and as I knock, excited voices envelop me, tumbling all around in a cacophony that tugs at my heart. When Milos answers, desperation in his warm brown eyes, I'm in his arms before I can even say hi.

"Thank God," he whispers in my ear. "I need your help."

"Don't just stand there, Milos! Invite her in." The woman's voice carries weight, and Milos closes his eyes for a moment before the barest shake of his head. Two children under the age of eight crowd around him.

"Uncle Milos, is this her?"

"She's pretty—you're pretty." The smaller girl, with a red bow tied in her hair, grabs my hand and tugs. "Come and have hot chocolate with us."

Milos gently removes her tiny fingers from mine. "Alesia, go find your mama. I need a moment with Elora." He squeezes into the hall with me and shuts the door behind him.

Stepping into his warm embrace again, all the panic I carried fades away. There are perks to dating a bodyguard: he knows how to protect me—even if he's protecting me from his own family. As we kiss, his tongue dancing with mine, his hands sliding down to squeeze my ass, I melt, and whatever assistance he needs, I'll give.

I note the strain he carries in the set of his shoulders and between his brows as we part. "What's wrong?"

"Elizabeth's tailor broke her ankle. The woman was supposed

to come to the house today to do the final fitting, but she can't leave her home. Elizabeth has to go to her. Mr. Fairhaven and Thomas are picking his mother up from the airport, and Samuel is on his way to Cambridge for the Christmas goose. I'm the only one available to take her. If I leave my family alone, they'll take over my apartment. I won't be able to find anything when they leave. Or, they'll try to get themselves back to the hotel alone. They know *nothing* of Boston. You should have seen them when we went out for breakfast this morning—they got lost four times *inside* the T-station."

"Can't someone else drive Elizabeth? They don't have a car service?"

"Mr. Fairhaven pays me well, Elora. Too well. He put my family up in their hotel, gave me extra time off... I can't say no when Elizabeth needs me for a few hours—especially not for her dress fitting just a week before the wedding. I hate to ask. But can you see my family back to the hotel? I'd take them now, but my mother is preparing the *dolmades* for tomorrow, and she has to finish them. The grape leaves are already steamed. If you could stay here for half an hour, and then call them a car..."

Half an hour with Milos's family? Alone? His mother must know of me—the teenage me who embarrassed my parents and had to be sent away. What will she think of me? Greek mothers are a breed all their own, and if Anna Sagona takes a liking to me, I'll be helpless to resist. But if she doesn't...this could be the longest half hour of my life...and could damage any possibility for a future with this man I've fallen for.

My heart wants to help, but fear cracks around the edges, and as I try to come up with a response that won't make me look like an ass, the door opens.

"Milos, are you going to introduce your young woman? Or hide her away?" His mother's cheeks carry a flush from cooking, and she wipes her hands on her apron.

Shoulders hunched, a muscle in his jaw ticking, Milos curves an arm around my waist. "Elora, this is Anna, my mother."

She looks me up and down. "You don't look like a vampire, *paidi mou*. Come inside. I need to add the seasonings to the lamb. Join me."

"Please," Milos whispers in my ear, a hint of desperation coloring his tone. "I will make it up to you. Anything you want."

Before I can answer, Anna takes my arm and leads me into the apartment. The dolma filling smells amazing, and within seconds, I'm plopped on a stool in front of a countertop of fresh herbs.

"Chop," she says.

Milos hovers behind me, waiting for an answer, while his sister, Isadore, introduces the rest of the family: his father Kipr and the young girls, Alesia and Dorianna—Dori for short.

"Go." I lean back so I can plant a quick kiss on his cheek. Though my nerves threaten to get the better of me, I can spend an hour with this loud, boisterous, happy family. Perhaps time with them will even relegate some of my most painful memories to the back of my mind, where they belong. "I'll make sure they get back to their hotel."

Relief eases the furrow between his brows, and he touches his forehead to mine. "Thank you, *glykia mou*."

Once he's gone, his mother pauses in her preparations and stares at me. "My son is smitten."

Oh God. I should have run when I had the chance. Still, I force a smile and try to ignore the dull ache spreading across my temples. "He's a good man. I..." What else do I say? I like him? I'm falling for him? I settle on a safe answer. "He means a lot to me."

Anna snorts. "You love him—or will soon. I see this in your eyes. In how you touch him."

Panic flares. This was a bad idea. The knife in my hand wobbles, so I set it down next to the neat piles of herbs. "We've... only been together...a short time."

"So?" Anna scoops up the herbs and dumps them into the

bowl with the lamb and the eggs. As she begins to stir, she clucks her tongue. "Love finds you when the time is right. I fell in love with Kipr the first day we met. Now, forty-two years later—"

Kipr shuffles into the kitchen. "I heard my name." As he wraps his arm around his wife's waist and plants a kiss on her cheek, the tenderness makes my heart ache.

"Your family must hate you being so far away on Christmas." His accented words slam into me, and I can't help flinching. "What is it?" He releases Anna, his bushy eyebrows drawn down with concern.

"I don't talk to my family. They never forgave me for the...uh... vampire thing."

Kipr's eyes harden. "You were what? Fifteen?" At my nod, he continues, "Fifteen-year-olds are idiots. All of them. When I was fifteen, I stole my father's car. With Anna. Isadore eloped. Or tried to. Milos drank so much at a party, we had to take him to the hospital to get his stomach pumped. And I found Tethys, our youngest, in jail after he broke into his school. No parent should abandon their child for a mistake at fifteen."

My eyes burn. He's right, and I've made that argument to my father a dozen times over email—with no response. I suppose all of those profanity-laced tirades over the phone in college didn't help. "Thank you." I can barely get the words out, and Kipr rounds the counter so he can take my hand.

"You have a new family now. You will see how the Sagonas celebrate Christmas." He winks at Anna. "I told you we would need that second bottle of ouzo."

Kipr is a large man—like his son—with salt-and-pepper hair and a nose that must have been broken at least once, but his smile...there's nothing but warmth there. As he limps back to the living room—the arthritic shuffle of one with poor knees or hips, I wonder how much longer I can pretend to be okay in the face of a family who's adopted me less than ten minutes after meeting me.

"You are good for Milos," Anna says, then sniffs at the bowl, adds another handful of herbs, and resumes stirring.

I'm not.

My greatest fear, that one day I'll hurt this wonderful, strong man I feel so much for, has my hands shaking, and I try to hide my nerves, but Anna's dark gaze seeks mine, and whatever she sees makes her set down her bowl, wipe her hands, and come to sit next to me.

"Why are you so frightened, Elora?"

"I'm sorry, Mrs. Sagona—"

"Anna."

I nod and force a smile. Dori and Alesia run circles around Kipr's chair in the living room, giggling the whole time, and Isadore tries to keep them from crashing into Milos's television every turn. The sounds of such a happy, close family bring tears to my eyes, and I blink hard to keep them from spilling over.

"How much do you know about my family?" My voice cracks, and Anna takes my hand.

"Enough that I would give your father a piece of my mind if I saw him on the street." She swears under her breath in Greek—something about stupidity and goats—and I choke out a laugh. "Is that why you didn't want to come? Because you thought we'd label you a vampire?"

Dropping my gaze to her hand on mine, I wonder if my own mother's hand would look much different after all of these years. "No," I manage. "Though you'd be the first Greek family not to, I think."

Anna captures a reddish lock of hair and tucks it behind my ear. "The old stories exist for a reason. Because people were frightened of what they did not understand. Anyone who believes red hair makes a woman a vampire is an idiot who has never heard of genetics. *I* am not an idiot."

Her indignation tugs at the corners of my lips. "I made a lot of mistakes growing up. And I lost my family. This," I gesture towards the children, who've both climbed into Kipr's lap while Isadore collapses on the couch, "is something I'll never have."

With a frustrated *hrumph*, Anna shakes her head. "Never? I see how my son feels about you. Everyone does. And though you fight it, I see how you feel about him too. Come for Christmas. You will see. Family is not always defined by blood."

Shaking my head, I lose control of a single tear. "I can't."

"Why not?"

I don't have a good answer, and when Anna slides off the stool and wraps her arms around me, I think maybe...*maybe* I can do this. Pretend. For a single day, I can believe I have a family.

"Spend Christmas with us, Elora. You would make Milos very happy. The rest of us too. Please," she says quietly as I struggle not to cry.

Unable to trust my voice, I nod, and she draws back with a smile that makes her look ten years younger. "Then we need to finish up these dolmades, don't we?"

This is a mistake. I wish I had the words to make her understand. But when Kipr starts reading the children a story, and Anna hums Christmas carols as she spreads the grape leaves out on cookie sheets, I shove my fears down deep—for Milos and for me.

Thirty minutes later, the dolmades are done and cooling on racks in the fridge, I've put Milos's gift under the tree, and Anna has somehow convinced me to take the family shopping before heading back to the hotel. "We do not need a car. The subway is fine. On the way, we will go find something special for Milos." She pats my arm. "And the children want to see the big Christmas tree. Can we go there, too?"

Why not? Boston Common and Copley Place aren't that far from one another. Or from their hotel. Alexander must have spent a mint on those rooms given their convenience to all the tourist attractions. We bundle up, and the kids insist that I help them with their mittens and button their coats for them before we head for the T. Getting five foreigners through the turnstiles and onto the train proves a feat worthy of Galileo, particularly since Dori won't let go of my hand. Silence is an unheard of phenomenon with this family, but my heart aches for the warmth they show one another—and me.

My grandmother's words come back to me now. *"Your father does not wish to see you."* I made a fucking mistake—a childish, stupid, rash mistake. Haven't I served my time? I'm distracted from my thoughts by a small mitten slipping into my hand. Dori motions me down to her level. My leg aches as I try to squat, but her eyes shine with exuberance, so I hide my wince with an over-eager smile.

"Are you going to marry Uncle Milos?"

No? Not yet? Maybe? If I say no, she'll get the wrong idea. And what if she tells Milos I said no? I don't want to hurt him, but we're brand new. Three weeks. "I don't know, *paidi mou*. We haven't known each other long. That's a question for much later, okay?"

"Like after church tonight?"

Oh, to be a child again and take everything so literally. "No, Dori. Like months from now. A long, long time." Her little face twists into a frown. "I like your uncle very much. But that's a grown-up question we need to think about." Desperate for a distraction, I straighten her little knit hat. "Now I have a question for you. What's on your Christmas list this year?"

The kids prattle on for the rest of the ride. Kipr watches over us while Anna and Isadore attempt to grill me about my life. They love the necklace I'm wearing, practically screaming when I admit I made it, and I wonder what I have at home I could bring over for Christmas. Something sparkly for the girls, understated for Anna and Isadore. How did I find myself here? Planning gifts for a family I barely know? Yet, we share common ground—Milos —and they're so like the idealized version of my own family that I've let myself buy in to the illusion that one day, I could have this again.

The train lurches, and a halo of light flashes behind Alesia's head. *Shit.*

My promise holds me, so I fish a pill out of my purse and swallow the tablet dry. *Please, not today. Let me get through the next few hours, and then I promise I'll do nothing for the rest of the day but sleep.* My bargaining doesn't usually work, but still, I try.

We spill onto the street at Boston Common, and the kids *ooo* and *ahh* at the tree, bright and shimmering against the early evening sky. A sprinkling of snow swirls around us, and for a moment, the world calms. I marvel at the beauty of my city and her people. Families glide onto the ice rink, and when the children beg to join them, Isadore promises an ice skating trip on the twenty-sixth.

Kipr takes my arm as we climb the steps to Copley Place. His broad shoulders and deep blue eyes paint a portrait of strength, but the stairs give him trouble. My right leg wobbles on the third step, and pain explodes across the back of my skull. As I hit the ground, my knee throbs, my vision going white. All around me voices clamor until Anna's call cuts through the din.

"Elora? Look at me, *paidi mou.*" She pats my cheek, and I realize I'm sitting, Kipr at my back, the girls crying next to Isadore. "We are going to call an ambulance."

"No," I whisper. "I just hurt my marshmallow and a few miles of sleep."

"What? Isadore, *ti léei aftí*? I do not understand. What does she want?" Anna's worried face swims in and out of focus.

"Seizure. Words aren't jacket well." Shit. I know I'm not making any sense. Offering my wrist, I hope they'll see the MedicAlert bracelet. "Home. Need...home."

Isadore flips the little medallion over. "Mama, it says she has epilepsy."

I struggle to get up, but Anna presses down on my shoulders. "Sit. Isadore, call your brother." As Anna rubs my chilled fingers, I fight against my tears. I can still conjure the memory of my mother comforting me—back before I irrevocably damaged that relationship forever.

Kipr takes the phone from Isadore. "Milos, she fell, and we don't understand what she's saying. Something about marshmallows and jackets."

He listens, then nods in response, waving off a woman who asks if we need help. "We will take care of her. You don't worry." Holding the phone close to my ear, he says, "She can hear you now."

"Elora? You don't have to answer me. I'm sending Thomas to pick you up and take you home. I will be there as soon as I can."

The strain in his voice sends my tears streaming down my cheeks, and I struggle to try to reassure him. "Don't basket," I say, then shake my head. "Sorry. Okay. Am...okay."

"Just rest. Promise me. And put Papa back on."

I nod, struggle to say Kipr's name, and eventually give up and gesture weakly to him to take the phone back. Anna and Kipr each grab hold of an arm and help me up and over to a bench, where a security guard brings me a cup of water. The children press themselves into my sides and wrap their arms around my waist. A tear slips down my cheek, followed by another, and another. By the time Thomas finds us, I've soaked my scarf, and I'm lucky my nose isn't the color of Rudolph's.

Walking proves difficult, so Thomas and Kipr support me, and soon we're all tucked into a warm limo, where I let my head rest against Anna's shoulder and fall asleep.

I barely notice being helped from the car, up the stairs, and into my bedroom. By the time my mind clears, I'm tucked into bed complete with pajamas, a result of Anna and Isadore's assistance. When little Dori brings me a cup of tea and cookies, so proud of not spilling a drop, I hear Kipr's words. *"You have a new family now."*

My small apartment fills with the sounds of that family. I smell soup, so like my mother's recipe, I can imagine her hovering over my stove. I hear Alesia's laughter as Isadore teases her and wonder what Darian's daughter looks like. Cracks form in my heart, fissures I thought long sealed. This family cares for me after knowing me for an hour, and my own family hasn't said two words to me in years. Dori climbs into bed with me and snuggles up. "I don't want you to be sick."

I'm in danger of falling in love. With Milos *and* his family. My emotions overwhelm me, vying with exhaustion. "I'll be okay, *paidi mou*. You took good care of me."

She proceeds to tell me a story, something about unicorns, and I close my eyes, letting the voice of a small child carry me back to my youth when Darian would read me stories—or create his own—to try to make me feel better.

Anna brings me a bowl of soup on a tray. "Dori, go help your mother with the dishes."

"But I want to stay with Elora," she whines, and her shrill voice renews the pounding in my head.

"No, *paidi mou*. Elora needs rest." Anna gently removes Dori's arms from my waist and pulls her from the bed. "You can see her before we leave."

Okay." Dejected, she trudges from the room, but not before she kisses my cheek. How can I do this? Be part of this family when all I want to do is have *my* mother here? My grandmother. Even my father.

When we're alone, Anna scoots closer and smoothes the blankets. "Soup will help. Isadore made enough for several meals."

The scent of the traditional chicken soup, spiked with lemon, fills the room, and with Anna here, I can taste my mother's recipe, feel her warm embrace. Every time I had a seizure as a child, she'd make *avgolemono*, and now, though years and heartache have tarnished the memories, I long for home.

Tears line my eyes, lending a shimmer to the world around me. "You've been so nice. And you don't even know me."

"I know Milos. He adores you, Elora, and I believe you feel the same. We are family now. What else can we do? Are you sure you don't need a doctor?"

If only a doctor could ease the pain of my memories, repair the relationship with my mother, make my father love me again. I close my eyes, and I can hear my mother singing to me, trying to calm me enough so I can sleep. No. Not my mother. Oh God. Anna sings the same lullaby I grew up with, and my tears spill once more, turning into hiccupping sobs as Anna wraps her arms around me, rocking me gently as she continues the song.

Too weak to push her away—physically and emotionally—I hold on to the memory, to the comfort of a mother's embrace, until my heart shatters, the agony overwhelming me and drawing a whimper from my lips.

"Milos said he will be here in half an hour, but I do not think we should wait. You need a doctor." Anna reaches for my phone, but I stop her, and when I meet her loving gaze, I can't pretend any longer.

"No." The word escapes on a sob. "I just need to rest. And...to be alone. I can't...do this. Be part of your family. I'm too broken. It hurts too much. Please..."

"You are not broken, Elora. You have been hurt by the people who should love you most. They do not deserve a daughter such as you. You are family now, and family accepts all the broken pieces." Anna's passion is infectious, and I wish I could change my mind—if only because she's everything I've always wanted in a mother—at least the little I've seen of her. A protector, a mediator, a kind and caring woman who puts others first and loves her children unconditionally. But no amount of wishing is going to make her words come true, and the more time I spend around these wonderful people, the more I realize how much I've lost.

My head throbs. "Please, Anna. You...all...you've been so wonderful, but I can't...I can't lose any more, and it's better this way..." I'm bawling now, and Anna nods, defeat marring her features. Yet she leans down and embraces me, and if I wasn't broken before, I'm thoroughly shattered now. I hold on for as long as I can, and when she pulls away, I'm sure I hear my heart crumble into dust.

"We will go, *paidi mou*. I hope once you've had a rest, you will change your mind." Her lips press into a thin line for a brief moment, but then she takes my hand. "Milos expects you for Christmas. Please do not break his heart."

Anna leaves me as a tear shines in her eye. I'm spared Isadore and Kipr, but the children won't go without hugs and more tears —mine, not theirs. When the door snicks shut, I call Milos.

"Elora? I'm leaving Elizabeth's now." His voice breaks, and I hate that I'm taking the coward's way out. But I've never felt more like the broken doll, and Milos deserves better.

"Don't come."

"What? Why not?"

"I can't do this, Milos. I'm sorry. You're such a good man, and I care about you, but I can't be who you need. Go be with your family. Please. They just left—they're getting a cab back to their hotel. I'm sorry. Please tell them I'm sorry. But...this was a mistake." I manage not to dissolve into tears as I grip the phone hard enough I'm afraid I'll crack the glass. "You deserve more."

He protests—or at least I think he does—but I end the call and let the phone slip from my hand.

I feel like a complete ass, but at least this way I'll eventually be able to piece my heart back together. Still, as I slide down under the blankets and lose my battle against my sobs, I fear I'll never be whole again.

9

Milos

*D*espite her message, I knock on her door less than half an hour later. "Elora? Please. Let me in." Another knock, this one harder, and I can't stop my hands from shaking. When I hear nothing from inside, I text her.

Sweetheart, please let me in. I need to see you.

Unwilling—or unable—to leave, I slide to the ground, my back against the wall, watching her door. Ten minutes later, I call her, barely able to speak when her voice mail picks up. "I don't 'deserve more.' I have everything I want and need with you, Elora. Please answer the door."

Five minutes after that, I repeat my plea in text, then with the lump in my throat steadily growing, I trudge down to the car, then head back to my apartment.

"Did you see her?" Mama demands the minute I walk through the door.

"No," I snap, but my frustration turns to sadness as soon as Mama wraps her arms around me. "What happened? She was...

happy when I left." I pull back, scanning my mother's face for answers. "Wasn't she?"

With a sigh, Mama pulls me into the living room. Isadore and the girls are back at the hotel, but Papa sits in the recliner, frowning.

"Milos," Mama says, "your Elora is scared."

"Of what?" I don't understand.

Papa clears his throat. "Of love."

"That's…" I want to say that's ridiculous, but then I think back to how frightened I was when I told her about the man I killed. "I have to fix this."

Squeezing my hand, Mama says, "I don't know that you can. Elora must decide if love is worth the risk."

The next day, my tiny apartment is full of the sounds of family, but I feel empty inside. Dori and Alesia keep asking me about Elora. "What's elipesy?" Alesia asks.

"Epilepsy, *paidi mou*," I tell her as I lift her up so she can pluck a candy cane from the top of the Christmas tree. "You remember when *giagiá's* car did that funny thing where the headlights kept flashing for no reason?"

"Yes," she says emphatically with a firm shake of her head. "*Giagiá* said the car had a ghost in it."

I shoot my mother a pointed look, but she just smiles, a little sadly. Turning my attention back to Alesia, I sink down on the couch with her on my lap. "It wasn't a ghost, little one. It was an electrical fault. The switch that controls the lights tried to talk to the lights, but the lights didn't want to listen. Epilepsy is when your brain has too much electricity bouncing around inside and, for a few minutes, it can't control your body."

"Is that why Elora couldn't say some words?"

I swallow hard, the lump in my throat a now-permanent addition. "Yes. She knew what she wanted to say, but the wrong words came out."

"Is she going to be okay?" Dori climbs up next to us and lays her head against my arm.

"Yes, baby. She'll be okay."

I just don't know if I will.

Elora

Christmas dawned hours ago with a fresh snowstorm, and I sip my coffee in front of my tree, the drapes thrown wide so I can see the brilliant white in the courtyard. I listened to all of Milos's voicemails and read all of his texts, and my eyes are so swollen from crying, I feel like someone punched me. I hope his family doesn't hate me.

I'd hate me.

White Christmas plays on the television as I unwrap a box of chocolates and a leather journal from my college roommate, Morgan. When Bing Crosby finds the carousel horse from Rosemary Clooney, the memory of Milos's arms around me, cuddling on the couch as we watched the same scene less than a week before, sends me over the edge, and I head for the shower so I can ignore my tears.

A little after two, a tentative knock rouses me from my daze. I catch my toe on the carpet on the way to the door, which flusters me enough that I forget to check the peephole.

"Elora." Milos holds a paper bag, and the scents of chow mein and kung pao chicken tickle my nose. I haven't eaten, and my stomach decides to let me know, loudly.

"What are you doing here?" I can barely hear my own voice. Shrinking back, I unwittingly give Milos the opportunity to step inside, and he shuts the door before he reaches for me.

"No. Please, Milos. I can't."

"You owe me an explanation. A real one." Without waiting for me to respond, he heads for my kitchen and unpacks the Chinese food. But that's not all he's brought. Two plastic containers have red ribbons tied around their green lids, and each has a construction paper card—one from each of the girls. "My mother made you *kourambiedes* and *dolmades*. She is worried about you. Dori and Alesia told me to hug you and make you better."

"I don't deserve this."

His shoulders hunch. "Maybe not. You hurt them, but family forgives, Elora."

As Milos runs a hand through his hair, I focus on the dark circles smudging his eyes, the way he's braced to absorb a blow, and my heart aches. I've done this. Ruined his Christmas. Hurt the nicest family I've ever met. Drove the man I lov—no. I don't love him because I can't. I'm too broken to love.

Except I do.

"Why?" He rests his hands on his hips, waiting for an answer I don't know I can give.

"Because it hurts too much." The words escape before I can think, each one a dagger to my shredded heart. Unable to stop myself, I dissolve into fresh tears, and Milos pulls me close. I lose myself in the scent of him. "Shh, *agápi mou*. I'm here. I'm here." He repeats his chant in Greek, and when he tells me he loves me, whispering, "*S 'agapó*," I shatter.

I don't remember leaving the kitchen, don't know how we got to my bed, but he's kissing me, and I don't want him to stop. Desperate hands pull at my clothes, and when I'm bared to him

—body and soul—he kneels, and his eyes glisten with tears. "You are my heart, Elora."

Deft fingers teasing my center stop me from speaking, and I'm lost to the building pleasure that carries me from one plateau to the next, higher and higher until I'm sure I'm floating in mid-air. When his mouth replaces his fingers, I fly apart, and he holds my hips, consuming me, setting fire to the one emotion I can't trust, the one that's hurt me so many times.

Hope.

As he enters me, I wrap my legs around him, too afraid of what's coming to risk letting go. Love smolders in his eyes, and as he whispers my name, I'm powerless to look away. Under my hands, the muscles of his back flex. As he thrusts deep, my nipples scrape against the coarse hair of his chest, sending me diving off the cliff once more. When he shouts my name and loses himself to me, I surrender to that hope, and as he collapses next to me, pulling me close, I wonder how I can survive what happens next.

"Come back with me," he says against the top of my head. "My mother has made a feast. Spend the rest of the day with us. Please." Emotion thickens his voice, and I can't stay in his arms or I'll lose my resolve.

I start to shake and pull away, drawing the sheet over my naked body. "I can't."

"Why not?" He watches me, his head propped on his hand. I trace the tattoo across his right pectoral muscle. The insignia for the Hellenic Armed Forces—the motto speaks of freedom and valor. "Elora, I love you."

The words mean more—and carry more pain—now that I'm not crying. Men will say anything to stop a woman's tears, and though I know Milos wouldn't lie to me, hearing the truth and the depth of his feelings only confirms my decision. I have to do this. I can't let him waste his life or his beautiful heart on me.

In the space of a breath, I try to memorize everything about him: the way he smells like the forest after a rainstorm; the deep timbre of his voice; how his stubble rasps beneath my fingers, against my thighs; the scar that bisects his oblique; his tight ass—even his hair. I won't see him like this ever again, and I want my memories to carry me through.

"I can't be with you, Milos." Unable to look at him, I sit up and turn away. "I can't love you." I do, though. More than I thought possible. But I can't let him see that. I'll only end up hurting us even worse than I am right now.

He reaches for me, but I scoot off the bed, snatch up his shirt, and throw the soft material at him. As I do, I catch a whiff of his scent, and dammit, I can't let myself cry.

This will protect him. And that's what you do for the people you love, right? And what my family never did for me.

He's too smart for me, though. "Can't? I'm sure you can love me, Elora. You just won't. You're too scared of being hurt. Did you ever think that maybe...I wouldn't hurt you?"

"That's not it!" I pull on my sweatshirt and fleece pants. I owe him the truth, and as much as I'd like to run away, to kick him out and hide behind a locked door, I can't. "Every minute I spent with your family hurt me, Milos. They're so wonderful. They took care of me, didn't even blink when I kept mixing up words or couldn't stand on my own. Your sister made me soup."

"And? This is a bad thing? They can be overbearing, but they live an ocean away." Milos buttons his pants and then frowns, frustration hunching his shoulders. "Please tell me you're not breaking up with me because you can't accept someone caring for you."

I fight my urge to turn away. "Every time Dori hugged me, I couldn't think of anything but my own family and how they threw me away—how I burned bridge after bridge until my father wouldn't even take my calls. Did you know that I called my *giagiá* the other day? She broke her hip two years ago. Darian, my little brother, has a four-year-old daughter! I didn't even know he got married! How can I be with you...be a part of your family... when I can't even talk to my own? It's too hard."

"Life is hard, Elora. I watched one of my closest friends die last year. I killed a man, and I see his face, see the life fade from his eyes every night. But that doesn't stop me from doing my job, from making new friends, from living. I thought it would. Until I met you. Then I realized that I'd risk all of that pain, and more, to have you in my life."

Anger flares up, white-hot and all-consuming. "I'm a coward. Is that what you want to say? Because you're right. I am. But this is my life, Milos. My pain. And you don't get to judge me for it. Go home. Be with your family. Tell them I'm sorry. That they're the best people I've met in a long time...other than you."

He reaches for me, seems to think better of the action, and lets his arm fall. Without another word, he leaves, and when my apartment door slams shut, Milos takes my heart with him.

10

Elora

*E*lizabeth assures me that Milos has the day off, but I'm still approaching panic when I knock on her door two days after Christmas. My phone has remained eerily silent, and given how often Milos and I texted—and sexted—in our last week together, the absence of any contact is a constant reminder of what I've lost. But I caused this, so I must live with the consequences. Samuel welcomes me inside and takes my arm as he leads me into the parlor.

"Miss Elora, are you all right?"

I clench my hands into fists and try not to let him see the tremble in my fingers. Does he know what happened? He works with Milos, but do men talk like women do? "I'm fine. I didn't sleep much last night."

"Or the night before that, I suspect." Samuel pauses, and the sympathy in his tone touches me. "He told me. I'm very sorry."

I nod my thanks and busy myself arranging a black velvet cloth on the coffee table. Elizabeth and Alexander's rings gleam in the overhead lights, and I withdraw a polishing cloth to touch up the gold and remove any lingering fingerprints. Despite my sorrow, pride inspires a small grin.

"Your work is brilliant, Elora." Alexander appears at my elbow. I have to shift so I can see him properly, and when I do, I knock over my bag, sending lip gloss, phone, and journal tumbling onto the floor. The two hand-drawn cards the girls made for me slide across the polished wood, and I spring forward, bang my knee against the table, and wind up on my ass, clutching the two drawings to my chest. With silent efficiency, Alexander gathers up all of my remaining things, returns them to my bag, and offers me his hand.

"Thank you. I'm afraid I'm a little jumpy today. That second cup of coffee wasn't a good idea." I try to laugh my way out from under his stare, and Alexander urges me back down on the couch.

"Elizabeth often reminds me that I tend to be a 'control freak,'" he says with a wry smile. "But may I offer some male perspective?"

This is not how I wanted the morning to go. But the love I've seen him show Elizabeth is heartwarming, so I nod and try not to let my lip wobble.

"Fear is any relationship's worst enemy. I don't know what happened. Nor will I pry or take sides. Milos is a trusted member of our household. I do not know you well, but Elizabeth considers you a friend, and I know you've helped her deal with some of her fears of late. If your relationship with Milos ended because of fear—I offer only this advice, which has served me well in business and my personal life for years. Think of the worst outcome, then ask yourself if that possibility carries the risk of more pain than you feel right now."

"I don't know," I say and look down at the cards in my hands. "But I miss him."

Alexander rests a hand on my shoulder. "Then perhaps you should tell him that. I'll bring you some tea."

With a few minutes to myself, I stare at the drawings. Alesia, the younger girl, drew flowers of every shape and size. Some of them even resemble actual flowers. Her five-year-old scrawl wishes me a "Mary Kristmas," and I trace the jagged lines of the text. Dori, at almost seven, has some budding talent. The Boston Christmas tree towers over the ice rink, and the sky twinkles with stars. Along the bottom of the page, she printed her name, and when I read her words on Christmas, I wondered how many times in one day a heart could break. *Don't be sad. You'll get better, and you can come skating with us.*

Simple, yes, but knowing the girls welcomed me so easily leaves me questioning how I could hurt them in a similar fashion. They'll get over it. Hell, they probably won't even remember me once they go back to Greece.

But Anna and Kipr treated me like a daughter.

"Dori can write beautifully for a seven-year-old." Elizabeth skirts the couch and takes a seat next to me. "Milos brought them by yesterday. The girls kept asking him about you. I think they were disappointed when I showed up instead." She smiles, and when she takes my hand, there's understanding in her touch.

Alexander returns with Samuel trailing behind bearing mugs of tea for all of us. When I've composed myself slightly, I force a smile and offer Alexander's ring first. He admires the intricate whorls and the etching that took me an entire day to perfect, runs his finger over the diamonds, and then slips the ring on his finger. "What do you think, *chérie?*"

Elizabeth's lower lip wobbles for a moment before she meets his gaze. "I think I can't wait to marry you." She lays her hand against his cheek, and the two share a brief, but intense kiss, bringing a flush to my cheeks. Elizabeth's ring fits perfectly as well. Rather than a thick circle like Alexander's ring, I've designed hers in a gentle *v*. Her engagement ring notches snugly, but if she chooses to wear the wedding band alone, she won't look like she's missing half of the ring.

"My grandmother would love this," she whispers. "She and my grandfather had forty years together, and when she died, she left me her ring so I'd find true love."

"I wish you'd have let me—and Ben—bring a lawsuit against your parents." Alexander squeezes her hand, and a muscle in his jaw ticks.

"I don't want any contact with them. They're not my family. You are. Nicholas. Kelsey and Toni. Terrance. I found true love, and as much as I wish things had been different, I'm happy. I don't need the actual ring—I have her spirit, thanks to Elora."

When they've reluctantly removed their rings, I polish them again, set them in silk-lined boxes, and hand them off to Samuel for safekeeping. "I'm afraid I have to head into the office for a few hours," Alexander says. When we rise, he leans in and buses my cheek. "We'll see you at the wedding?"

The entire day, I've dreaded that question. I can't go, as much as I'd like to. Elizabeth is such a lovely person. Genuine, kind, and completely down to earth, despite who she's going to marry —and her personal wealth. Rumors are she got a high six-figure settlement from the brouhaha last year. Alexander confirmed we're on the road to being friends. Heaven knows I've spent enough time with her over the past few weeks. But Milos will be there, and seeing him—I can't. I just can't.

"N-no. I'm afraid I can't attend. I want to. Really. But—"

Elizabeth silences me with her hand on my arm. "Go take over the world," she tells Alexander. "Elora and I are going to have some lunch if she has the time." As she embraces him, she drops her voice to a whisper. "I'll sort this."

I should make some excuse to leave, but Elizabeth warps her arm around my shoulders and leads me into the formal dining room. "Sit. You and I are going to talk."

Her tone, firmer than I've ever heard her use, stills my

protests, and as she disappears into another room, my stomach churns with both hunger and nerves. I hope she's not going to try to fix what I broke: Milos's heart.

I'm sure you can love me, Elora. You just won't.

Elizabeth returns with a small box—the kind you store family photos in. "Donatella is making us grilled cheese sandwiches and tomato soup. But while she's doing that, I want you to see something."

Newspaper clippings rest on the top of the box, and at her gesture, I take the first one. The Seattle Times decried Bennett Pharmaceuticals for their pricing practices and cited an anonymous source for exposing a vast scheme of overcharging, internal memos more damning than any I've ever seen. "What is all of this?"

"I was the anonymous source, Elora. I worked in the accounting department, and after I found some of those memos, I went to my parents and begged them to change their ways. When they refused, I exposed them, and they disowned me."

"I'm sorry." I glance down at the paper, at the black and white text that brought about the end of a family—and gave Elizabeth freedom.

"Don't be. I'm better off without them. And without my former fiancé. He was an abusive asshole who wanted me to be his perfect little doll. He used to berate me for every bite of food I ate over what he deemed appropriate. He convinced me I was a worthless, fat, and uninteresting woman whose only redeeming quality was my looks. Even now, I still can't help my worry when Donatella makes french fries or soufflés. I pushed Alexander away because he tried to take care of me, knew what I needed—even when I didn't—and I couldn't trust any man after what Darren had done to me."

Her openness brings warmth to my cheeks as I peruse a typed letter she hands me. The vitriol shocks me, sends me back to my fights with my mother and father. No wonder she didn't want any contact with her mother. "I can't believe your mother sent this." I squeeze Elizabeth's hand and confess my own truth.

Elizabeth laughs when I tell her how I pretended to be a vampire as a young teen, but when I don't join in, she covers her mouth, and bright red spots bloom on her cheeks.

I can't stop talking now. The words pour out of me. "I haven't talked to my parents since college. I don't know how to be part of a family anymore."

"This is why you broke up with Milos?"

The mention of his name sends a tear sliding down my cheek, and I nod. "His whole family tried to help me after I had a seizure on Christmas Eve. They took care of me. Dori climbed into bed with me and told me a story. His mother sang me the same lullaby my mother favored. And I couldn't think of anything but what I've lost. He's a wonderful man. Patient and kind and perfect. But I'm broken. And he deserves better."

"We're all broken, Elora. Scarred. Afraid. But that's how we know we're alive. When Alexander pursued me, I pushed him away. Repeatedly. I didn't want anything to do with a man who could buy and sell a small country. I'd had enough of that life with my parents. He tried for weeks to convince me he was more than his bank account. Once I let him in, I realized that I'd judged him unfairly, and almost let my past pain preclude future happiness.

"Milos is one of the kindest men I've ever met. And the saddest. But these past few weeks, he's changed. Between you and his family, he was downright happy on Christmas Eve. But yesterday? I've never seen him so sad. I don't think he spoke a single word other than telling me you broke up with him because you were afraid to be happy."

Whatever part of my poor heart hadn't cracked before is done for now. "I never wanted to hurt him. These past few weeks have been the happiest I've had in years...but I can't—"

"I don't expect you to get back together with him because I

told you all of this. Or shared my mess of a family story with you. What happened between the two of you is your business. Not mine. But just think about what I've said. Sometimes the best things in life are born from pain. And sometimes, you have to make your own family."

11

Elora

*T*essa, my therapist, hands me a box of tissues. "Your mother hasn't called?"

"N-no." I'm not sure why this surprises me. Despite my grandmother's assurances she'd call, three days after Christmas, I'm still waiting. "She won't."

"What about Darian?" She scribbles in her notebook, and I wonder what she has to take notes on after several years together. We have a standing appointment the week after Christmas, though at least this year, I have new heartaches to tell her.

With a shrug, I stare down at my feet. "I don't even know his daughter's name."

She switches tactics. "Did Milos's family do anything wrong?"

"No! They were perfect." I dab at my eyes, the memory of Anna's lullaby haunting me, as she's haunted my dreams every night this week.

"And you had a good time with them before your seizure?" Her pen scratches the paper again, and she raises a brow.

I nod. "You don't have to tell me how stupid I was."

"You weren't stupid, Elora. Pain makes us do things we know we shouldn't. Like hurting those we love. But that's not stupidity. If anything, it's closer to fear. You sent his family away, sent Milos away, because you feared they would one day hurt you like your own family hurt you."

Only the deep cushions prevent me from falling out of my chair. For the past few days, I believed I pushed them away because I didn't want to deal with the memories of past pain, but with that single statement, Tessa opens a new wound, one that bleeds brighter than all the rest. "And what if they do?"

"What if they don't?"

I hate her a little right now. My scowl wobbles, my lower lip jutting out despite my best efforts to trap the tender flesh between my teeth. "It doesn't matter. I hurt them. Hurt him. He doesn't want anything to do with me."

"Do you love him?"

"Yes." No hesitation, no second thoughts. "He loved me, too."

"Love doesn't fade in three days, Elora. If you want to fix things, you can."

And with those words hanging in the air between us, I wonder how far I'd have to go to make things right.

Anna takes a seat across from me in the hotel's bar, and something in her gaze warns me she'll spare me little patience. The family leaves in the morning, and I'll probably never see them again, but I couldn't let them go without trying to explain—or at least apologizing one more time.

Gifts clutter the small table: necklaces for the girls, bracelets for Anna, Isadore, and Milos's other two sisters, Sasha and

Simone. For Kipr and Tethys, I chose sets of cufflinks with matching tie tacks, and I brought a set for Milos as well.

"You are feeling better?" Her voice doesn't carry the same warmth as the last time we spoke, and I don't blame her for protecting herself.

"Physically, yes." How do you tell someone about a lifetime of pain in a few minutes? Tessa's words come back to me. *If you want to fix things, you can.* "I'm sorry. I didn't mean to hurt any of you, least of all Milos." If I'm not careful, I'll lose my battle against tears yet again.

"Milos is the one you should apologize to, Elora."

"I know." I twist the ring on my thumb, the peridot twinkling in the overhead lights. "I caused the rift with my family, and I'll carry that guilt for the rest of my life. The lullaby you sang me after my seizure? My mother used to sing that same song."

Anna stares down at her hands, folded on the table and something in her expression softens. "I reminded you of her? Too much, then?"

"Yes, but that's not why I sent you away." I'm making a mess of this. Though, she's still here, still listening. "I love Milos."

"That is obvious." She smiles, and when she takes my hand, a few tears escape my control. "Why are you here with me, rather than him?"

Fear. If Anna rejects me, I'll drown my sorrows in ice cream and sappy movies for a few days and count the minutes until my next therapy session. Baring my soul to Milos has the power to destroy me. "I need time," I say, "but I will tell him. I couldn't let you go back to Greece without knowing why."

"Promise me." She leans forward, and her strong grip on my hands warns me she'll fly all the way back from Athens if I don't work up the nerve to talk to him soon. Greek mothers don't take no for an answer. "Do not wait too long, Elora. Love is precious, and when new, often fragile. I saw light in my son's eyes before you sent him away, but now, darkness lingers. He deserves to be happy. As do you. So promise me you will tell him soon."

"I promise."

The children won't be able to resist telling Uncle Milos that I came by, so I leave Anna to smuggle the gifts into her suitcase, for distribution once they're all back in Greece. When she says good-bye, we embrace, and just before I pull away, she whispers in my ear. "You are family, Elora. And families fight. But they also forgive. *Kalá Christoúgenna, paidi mou.*"

Merry Christmas.

Milos

The silence of my apartment shocks me. Leaving my family at the airport this morning was one of the hardest things I've ever done —so much harder than moving to the States, harder even than telling Mama about the man I killed, because now, I'm completely alone.

Once I've poured myself a beer, I sink down onto the couch and open the gift bag Mama handed me before she kissed me goodbye. "Not until you get home," she admonished.

Milos,

You have always made me proud. From the first day I held you, I knew you would be a great man. Seeing you happy, even for a few days, is the greatest gift I could have received. Elora came to see me yesterday to apologize. She loves you. I cannot say whether she will ever be able to tell you this, but I have seen the truth in her eyes. She left this for you, and I hope it brings you joy.

Love, Mama

The golden ribbon around the small box gives way, and I run

my fingers over the cufflinks. A single peridot winks from the corner of each one.

"Elora, please come back to me."

Elora

Laden down with boxes, I peer through the door of Artist's Grind. Thankfully, Devan sees me before I lose my grip, and when I'm safely inside, she relieves me of my load. "You've been busy."

I have. When you ruin your life, throwing yourself into your work helps. Or so I've tried to tell myself. Turns out, that's a lie, but at least I have something to show for my sleepless nights—something beyond dark circles under my eyes and sunken cheeks. Seeing Anna lifted the worst of the darkness, but though I know I have to apologize to Milos, I'm not sure I'm strong enough to do so. I spent hours the previous night working out what to say, even writing him a letter, but I have to see him in person, and I'm terrified.

"Elora, what's wrong?" Devan pulls me over to one of the corner tables. Only a couple of customers linger, tapping away on their laptops with mugs of coffee at their elbows. If I thought Devan would give up—or believe a lie—I'd blow her off, but she knows me better than anyone in this town.

"I broke up with Milos."

She listens as I recount the story, much as I'd told Elizabeth, but with more details about his wonderful family and how I probably overreacted.

Probably? Who am I kidding? I made overreacting an Olympic sport—and then took the gold medal.

"So fix it. Call him." Devan's so earnest, I almost believe I have a chance.

"I want to. But...if he rejects me..."

She rolls her eyes. "You'll be no worse off than you are right now. How many times have you cried since Christmas Eve?"

"It'd be easier to count the times I *haven't* cried."

"Then it's settled. You're going to get him back. Or try anyway. He'll be at Elizabeth and Alexander's wedding. Do it there. Mac and I will help." Devan nods, as if she's certain her plan will succeed.

"I don't want to cause any problems at the wedding. Elizabeth—"

Devan holds up her hand. "It's New Year's Eve, Elora. You'll be there at midnight. Do you really think he won't want to kiss you? I'm calling this 'Operation Auld Lang Syne.' By the end of the night tomorrow, you're going to have your man back."

For the first time in almost a week, I smile.

I hope she's right.

Devan insists we spend the morning before the wedding getting pampered. I'm not sure how she managed to wrangle two appointments for manicures, pedicures, and professional makeup applications on such short notice, but when I stand in front of my full-length mirror before I leave my apartment, I'm thankful she's such a miracle worker.

Elizabeth's colors are silver and gold, so I chose a dress in a deep blue, one I bought a few days before Christmas. The shimmery material hugs every curve. As an added benefit, the sexy corset underneath frames my breasts beautifully, and for once, I'm not self-conscious about my proportions.

Tucking a few tissues in my small clutch, I pray I won't end up fleeing the hotel in tears. In the next few hours, I'll know where I stand with the man I love.

The hotel gleams—every surface sparkles, and uniformed attendants direct guests to the grand ballroom. Silver and gold adorn every surface, ribbons decorating red poinsettias, sparkling gold tablecloths under silver chargers. Wet bars offering champagne, wine, and whiskey have small crowds gathered around them, and at the front of the room, Alexander's brother, Nicholas, chats with a lovely brunette and a man I don't recognize.

I scan the room. Devan and Mac showed up ten minutes before me so Devan could find Milos and get him away from the crowds. But when she rushes over to me, I start to panic. "He didn't come?"

"Calm down, Elora. He's outside with Mac." She points to glass doors that lead to a terrace. Milos huddles under a heater without an overcoat, his hands in his pockets, Mac at his side. "That's the look of a man who's lost everything. Go talk to him."

His dark suit strains across his broad shoulders, and I catch a glimpse of gold cufflinks at his wrists—the ones I gave him. The walk across the ballroom feels like it takes a year, and I slip through the door, barely able to breathe. Snowflakes dance along the terrace, but glass walls protect us, and as I tiptoe closer, warmth from the heater pulls me in.

"Milos?"

Shock jerks his shoulders, or perhaps that's pain, because when he turns to look at me, the anguish of the past week is etched into his handsome face. I can't look away from his eyes, which glisten, and the enormity of what I did to him—and to myself—almost sends me running away before I say another word. But Mac slips past me and gives my hand a quick squeeze. I can do this.

"What are you doing here?" Clipped words, devoid of any

emotion, land like icicles against my skin, and I take a step back. I deserve that and so much more.

Steeling myself for another blow, I straighten my shoulders. "I came to apologize."

Whatever he's expecting me to say, that wasn't it. "For? I can think of half a dozen different ways you hurt me and my family in the last week. Which one?"

"All of them." My voice falters, and as I take a step forward, my right knee wobbles, and I brace myself against one of the nearby tables. "I'm a coward, Milos. Your family tried to take care of me when they'd only just met me. They cooked for me, kept me safe...they *loved* me. And I couldn't accept their help because deep down, I wanted *my* family to do that for me."

Stronger now, I take another step so I'm only a foot away— close enough to smell his spicy scent and see a small shaving cut on his jaw. I've missed him so much this past week, and I have to tell him why. "I was afraid that if I let them in—let *you* in—that I'd have to carry that pain with me every day. I thought I'd moved on. Or at least dealt with the loss of my parents, my brother, my grandmother. But apparently not. At least, not completely."

He nods, and a bit of the ire fades, tiny lines around his full lips easing. His eyes haven't softened, though.

"Your father told me I had a new family within ten minutes of meeting me. And that terrified me. How could someone be so accepting? So willing to give love just because he knew I needed it?"

"That is how they are. My mother has a sixth sense. She can tell a good person almost immediately. If she likes you, you're family. And she knew from the moment she met you that you—" He stops and turns away, but I grab his forearm.

Hard muscles shift under my hand. "What did she know about me?"

"That you loved me."

Neither of us breathes as the words stretch out between us,

hanging in the air because I'm still too much of a coward to confess the last part of my truth.

"I had to tell her she was wrong."

I can barely hear the whispered words because, at that moment, Devan calls to us, and the music drowns out any courage I had left.

"I'm sorry, but the wedding's about to start." She meets my gaze, questioning, but I shake my head. I didn't have enough time.

Yet as we head back inside, Milos rests his hand on my lower back, guiding me to a seat in the second row. I can't ask him to stay with me, but he does, sitting stiffly beside me as the music swells and Elizabeth, dressed in a floor-length silver and gold gown with glittering diamonds at her throat, glides up the aisle.

Alexander watches, captivated, his black tuxedo finished with a silver vest, bow tie, and pocket square. The officiant introduces himself as a longtime friend of Alexander's, Terrance, and while he waxes poetically about love in all its forms, I think back to Anna's words.

You love him—or will soon. I see this in your eyes. In how you touch him.

I couldn't admit it then. I deflected, but now I know the truth.

"Alexander, you have vows you've written?" Terrance asks, and a small child hands Alexander the ring I made for Elizabeth.

He takes her hand and slips the ring on her finger. "Elizabeth, the first time I tried to take you to coffee, you stormed out after calling me a name I will not repeat in mixed company." The guests chuckle, and Alexander sweeps his gaze around the room. "The term 'control freak' has been bandied about more than once." More laughter as he turns back to his bride. "We've had our spats, and I remember your disbelief that someone like me could ever want someone like you. But all you saw—at least in the beginning—were my circumstances.

"I pursued you, long past the point of reason, because of your brilliant mind, your tender heart. You love unconditionally, you forgive easily, and your laugh is one of my favorite sounds in the entire world. You make me a better man, perhaps a bit less of a 'control freak,' and for that, I will spend the rest of my life worshiping you, honoring you, and above all, loving you."

Elizabeth dashes away a tear, her eyes shining. "Alexander," she says as she slides his band over his knuckle. "When we met, you frightened me. I thought you were pompous and entitled and so handsome it hurt to look at you." Elizabeth blushes and focuses on their joined hands for a moment before she continues. "And when you asked me to trust you, I couldn't help myself. From our first date, I knew my life would never be the same. You accepted the parts of me that I thought had been damaged beyond repair, helped me understand I wasn't broken—just bruised. With you, I found a home, a family, and above all, love. You're still a 'control freak,' and I wouldn't change that for the world. I love you."

I can't help myself. I reach for Milos's hand, and though he tenses, he doesn't pull away. As Terrance pronounces them husband and wife, Milos brushes a tear from my cheek. "Don't cry, *glykia mou*."

His tender words soothe my shattered heart, and I turn to him as Elizabeth and Alexander kiss. "I was a fool. Can you forgive me?"

Applause erupts around us, and Milos pulls me to my feet with the rest of the crowd. Elizabeth and Alexander look so happy, and as they make their way down the aisle, Milos wraps his arm around my waist. I link our fingers, desperate to strengthen the connection between us, hope flaring for the first time in a week, though still little more than an ember.

"I fell in love with you, Elora." I try to turn to face him, but Milos holds me still, his mouth inches from my ear. "No. Not yet. I need to finish. Dori told me you were scared. I didn't understand why. When you told me it hurt too much to be around my family, everything made sense. I want to be with you. More than I've wanted anyone before. But I can't change who I am. My family is important to me. I want you to be a part of that family. But if being with me is going to cause you pain, then I have to walk away. But know it will be the hardest thing I've ever had to do."

Love is precious, and when new, often fragile.

Anna's words haunt me. I waited too long.

12

Elora

*M*ilos rests his cheek against the crown of my head. "Stay here and enjoy the party. I'll make an excuse to Elizabeth and Alexander and go."

The moment he releases me, I spin around and grab his hand. "Outside. Now." He tries to pull away, but I inherited my glare from my grandmother, and no one messes with a Greek woman when she's mad. After I glare at him a second time, he allows me to lead him back out to the patio.

"I won't fight with you, Elora."

"Good. You never answered my question. Can you forgive me?" I should probably lower my voice—try to sound recalcitrant, but I'm over that now. I fucked up, worse than I've fucked up in years. But I'm not walking away. Not until I tell him how much I love him.

"I forgave you the moment I saw you tonight." Truth shines in his eyes as he shakes his head. "But that doesn't mean I can be with you. I won't hurt you again."

"Do you still love me?" My breath catches in my throat, and I grip the top of the chair next to me. His answer may be the most important one I ever hear, and I fight to blink back the tears that threaten to obscure my vision. I won't cry. Whatever he says, I'll accept. I'll have to.

If I thought he looked miserable at my apartment on Christmas, he looks ten times worse now. A single word scrapes roughly from his throat. "Yes."

When I throw myself into his arms, he catches me easily. "Elora."

"Now I'm the one who needs to finish." I trace a knuckle along his jaw, and he holds his breath. "All those reasons for pushing you and your family away? I left out the biggest one of all. Fear. My own family rejected me. Cast me out and never looked back. I couldn't let myself love you, couldn't accept your family's love and care because what if they rejected me too? I didn't think I'd survive a second time."

He starts to protest, but I silence him with a finger pressed to his lips. "Love is a risk. Maybe the greatest risk of all. And one I'm willing to take. I love you, Milos. I've loved you since Christmas Eve—and maybe even before."

"I don't want to cause you pain." He cups my cheek, and as his thumb brushes away a tear I can't hold back, he leans down to press a gentle kiss to my lips. His touch is home, and I rise onto my toes to deepen the connection between us. When we part, neither satisfied, but needing to come up for air, he frowns. "You are freezing."

At some point during the ceremony, the heaters must have shut down, but I don't notice the cold. Milos stokes the flames of my desire, along with the reassurance of something else: love. He sheds his suit jacket and drapes the black material around my shoulders. I snuggle into his warmth, enjoying the scent of him, the way his arms feel around me, and the muffled strains of the orchestra through the glass doors. "No one lives without pain,

Milos. I miss my family every day, but I won't let that stop me from loving you. Say you'll take me back. Please. I want to start the new year with you. And many more after this one."

Milos buries his face against my neck and feathers kisses all the way from my jaw to my ear. "Don't shut me out again, Elora. Whatever you're feeling, whenever you're scared or in pain, I need to know. Promise me."

I meet his intense gaze. "I promise. I love you."

Our kiss rocks me all the way to my toes, and suddenly, I'm no longer chilled, but on fire. His hand slides down to brush my ass, and he almost growls as he pulls me against his growing erection. "I have a room upstairs."

"Soon, *agápi mou*," I say. "I haven't been to a wedding in years. I want to dance with you." Wriggling out of his arms, I shake my ass at him as I flee back inside. Milos doesn't let me get far, and he pays me back by pinching my left butt cheek as he catches me. I try to retaliate, but my arms are quickly trapped when he holds his jacket shut.

"You don't fight fair!" I protest, but I can't help my laugh as he cages me against him.

"Just wait until later, love. I'll be quite fair. Unless you make me punish you."

I'm blushing when Devan and Mac join us. She leans in for a hug. "'Operation Auld Lang Syne' complete?"

I nod, and she turns her smile on Milos. "What are you two still doing here? Get a room."

"Elora wants to dance." Milos dips me, and I clutch his arms, laughing, until I find myself staring up into Elizabeth and Alexander's amused faces.

Once I'm set to rights, Elizabeth kisses my cheek and whispers, "I'm glad you seem to have worked things out."

Her wedding dress rustles as I hug her, and for the first time in a week, the tears I want to cry are those of joy, not pain. "You helped make this happen."

"No, Elora. You did this all on your own." Elizabeth practically glows as Alexander wraps his arm around her once more.

Milos, Mac, and Alexander laugh about something I missed, but there's no mistaking the love reflected in the men's eyes. A uniformed waiter with a tray of champagne flutes pauses, and we each lift a glass. "To love," Alexander says with his wife pressed to his side.

"To love." I can't help but smile as the bubbles tickle my throat. Milos's gaze smolders, and when the happy couple is called away for their first dance, I lean back against him, pondering just how long we have to stay before we can take advantage of that room.

Milos presses a kiss to the back of my neck. "'Operation Auld Lang Syne'?"

"You didn't think it strange that Mac wanted to talk outside? In the middle of winter?"

His laugh is one of my favorite sounds, second only to how he says my name, and I twist in his arms so I can see the light in his eyes and his smile. "I'd say Devan's plan was a smashing success."

"Definitely."

We laugh, dance, and drink the night away. I stick to the slow songs, holding onto Milos lest I fall on my face, but neither of us want to let go of one another. Even Mac dances a little, though his limp becomes more pronounced as the night goes on, and before long, he and Devan lounge at one of the tables against the wall, watching the revelers.

As midnight approaches, the uniformed waitstaff distributes fresh glasses of champagne, and Elizabeth and Alexander lead the countdown to the new year.

Milos holds me close, and we whisper our chant in tandem. As the clock rolls over and the guests erupt into applause, he leans in, and I hold my breath. I dreamed of this moment last night, and Milos doesn't disappoint, his kiss sending chills down to my toes.

After we say a hasty goodbye to Devan and Mac and wave to Elizabeth, we hurry to the elevator. But two couples join us, and we can do nothing more than link our fingers, though if I had my preference, I'd already have his shirt unbuttoned, my hand down his very nicely pressed pants.

By the time we reach his room, I'm so desperate to get his clothes off, I don't even wait until he's set the deadbolt to strip off his jacket. "I dreamed about you," I say between kisses. "Every night." As I unbutton his shirt, I meet his gaze. "Your kiss, your touch." The shirt hits the floor, and I press my lips to his shoulder. "The way you say my name."

"Elora." Milos cups my breast through the satin, and my nipples pebble, aching for his mouth. I reach for his tie, but he stills my hands. "No. Tonight, you are mine. Do you trust me?"

I nod, and he leads me to the bed.

"Close your eyes." Milos tucks a lock of hair behind my right ear. His warm breath tickles my cheek. "Do not move."

"And what if I do?"

He slides his hand down my dress, skimming my mound, and if my panties haven't melted from the heat between my legs, they soon will. I can't see, but I sense him, and he drops to his knees and slowly lifts my skirt. As his fingers dance along the seam of my thong, I can't help my whimper. The smooth pads of his fingers ease the black lace down my thighs.

"If you move, I won't be able to take my time, and you, *agápi mou*, deserve to be worshiped for hours."

As Milos feathers my inner thighs with gentle kisses, I try to hold still, but before long, I'm thrusting my hips towards him, begging for him to take me. I expect him to stop, to punish me somehow for my infraction, and I welcome his sweet torture. Instead, he wraps his arms around me and lays his cheek against my stomach. I risk a glance, and he meets my gaze. "I love you, Elora."

My dress has an odd catch under the arm, and I loosen the hook, slide the zipper down, and raise my brows. "Then make love to me, Milos. It's a new year. Let's have our new beginning."

With aching slowness, he slides my dress from my shoulders, and soon, I'm left in only my corset, the snug, black material holding me upright. Milos dips a finger into my wetness, and I push against him, but he won't let me come so soon. Secretly, I'm thrilled, and as he sweeps his tongue against my clit, I grab onto his shoulders to keep me upright.

"Lie down. The things I plan on doing to you tonight...you're not going to be able to stand for hours."

He positions me in the center of the bed, then removes his tie. Wrapping my wrists snugly, he hooks the tie on the headboard—who knew the Fairmont provided bondage hooks?—and then stands, his hungry gaze drinking in every inch of me.

"Please," I beg and squeeze my legs together to find some relief from the desire throbbing between my thighs.

I admire his chest as he strips off his shirt, his toned arms, the ink swirling over his bicep. A poem for his family, he explained last week, and one day I want to hear it, but for now, I'm too desperate for his hands and his mouth, and yes, his cock. I pull against my bindings, but despite the silky material, the knot holds. The confinement heightens every sensation, and when he sheds his pants and briefs and stands before me naked, I renew my plea.

Relenting, he settles between my legs. Hands on my hips, he holds me still as his tongue traces my lower lips. He knows exactly how to drive me higher, but never let me crest, and I can do nothing but writhe under his teasing kisses, his gentle nips to my inner thighs, his fingers as they dance along the very edge of where I so desperately need him to be. I cry out for him, and he stills, gazing up at me with the look of a man who's found his home.

"Please." Desperation edges my voice, and with a smile, Milos returns his attention to my clit, and my entire world dissolves into light and love and pleasure.

EPILOGUE

One month later

Elora

*T*hese have been the longest four weeks of my life. Milos guarded Elizabeth and Alexander during their honeymoon to Ireland, Scotland, and Wales. We kept in touch over Skype and text, and that forced us to slow down, to spend our time outside of the bedroom—for the most part. I won't deny the Saturday evening video calls that ended in some spectacular orgasms for both of us.

But now, while the happy couple is on a private cruise around the Greek Isles, Milos has a week off, and after a long flight to join him, we're in a car, rolling slowly down a street just outside Kallithea.

My heart skips a beat as an old woman shuffles out of a hole-in-the-wall restaurant and meets my gaze. Her smile and hunched posture remind me of my grandmother, and I brush away a tear. "I've missed this," I say as I roll down the window and inhale the unique scent of Athens in the winter. It's unseasonably warm, and the sea looks like glittering diamonds in the sun.

"And I have missed *you*." Milos brushes a knuckle along my jaw while we wait for a family with three small children to cross the street. "Are you certain you're ready for the entire Sagona family?"

"No." The tremble in my voice must worry him, for he quickly pulls over to the side of the road, then turns to me and takes my hands.

"What do you need, *agápi mou*? How can I make this easier on you?" Understanding wells in his dark brown eyes, and I hold on tight, needing the anchor of his fingers to stop my racing thoughts.

"Can we...stop for a coffee?"

Milos hurries around to passenger side of the car, then helps me to my feet. Between the jet-lag and our sensual reunion, I haven't slept much, and I sway a little until his strong arm pulls me close. The few blocks' walk revives me a bit, the balm of the sea air fortifying me for whatever comes next.

In a little corner coffee shop, Milos orders us drinks, and I try to hide my face behind my hair. It's been so long...but what if someone recognizes me?

Once we're seated at a small table, close enough for our knees to touch, he meets my gaze. "There's something else, isn't there?"

"I called my *giagiá* before I got on the plane." The words escape barely louder than a whisper, and I force myself to continue. "I...talked to my mother. For just a few minutes. Told her I was coming to Greece."

"What did she say?" He must suspect, for he cups my hands with his.

I shake my head. "She told me my father wouldn't want her talking to me. But..." Tears burn in the corners of my eyes. "She gave me Darian's email address. I don't know if he'll respond, but at least...there's a chance I could talk to my brother again."

Milos's smile warms me even more than the coffee. "If we need to stay an extra few days so you can see him...we will."

We. I don't know how or when *we* began, but sitting in a little corner shop with sweet, rich coffee, holding hands, and hearing the chatter of our native tongue all around us, *we* feel right.

An hour later, Milos parks at the bottom of a small hill. I'm nervous about seeing everyone, though Anna and I have talked twice now, and she assures me the whole family will love me.

The white cement walls need a good cleaning, but the small home, the one Milos and his four siblings grew up in, sits amid concrete planters filled with bright pink flowers. We have to climb a long set of steps to reach the house, and Milos takes my arm to help me. The hours of travel and the exhaustion have left me unsteady on my feet. My nerves don't help either.

An electric chair at the top of the steps gives Milos pause, though he knew his father's knees couldn't take the climb any longer. "I hate being so far away," he says as we approach the front landing.

I'm not ready. I claw at the neck of my sweater, the stirrings of panic sending my heart pounding, but then Dori throws open the bright blue door, and before I can even say "hi," she's wrapped her little arms around me. "You got better!"

Tears line my eyes as I return the embrace, and next to me, Alesia begs Milos to pick her up. He spins her in the air, and her shrieks of joy warm my heart. I'm pulled inside with more gusto than a child as small as Dori should be able to manage, with Milos and Alesia at my back.

The home is alive with the scents of seasoned lamb, a television blaring cartoons somewhere in the back, and loud, boisterous voices clamoring for Milos's attention. I hang back, with Dori at my side, until Anna shoulders her way through the throng of her children. "Elora, we're glad you came. Welcome home."

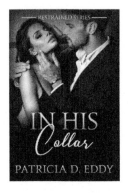

NICK FAIRHAVEN HASN'T PLACED a bet in eighteen months. Not since his gambling almost cost his sister-in-law her life.

But just because Nick's squeaky clean now, doesn't mean the world sees him that way.

Welcome to **IN HIS COLLAR**.

Control is an art form.

One Nick thought he mastered long ago. But gambling is a cruel mistress, and he lost everything.

A chance meeting gives him hope for redemption. Now, he's balanced on the knife's edge between the future he wants and the past he can't escape.

Will he risk it all for the woman he loves? Or will his life be nothing but unfulfilled promises?

One-click IN HIS COLLAR now!

IF YOU LOVED All Tied Up For New Year's, you'll love **BREAKING HIS CODE**, my sensual, geeky, and thrilling military romance.

She's a wounded warrior. He's a former SEAL and a hell of an online gamer. Can their love survive the transition to the real world?

After almost dying in an Afghanistan war zone, Cam found it easier to live in the virtual world than face reality. Until her flirtatious gaming buddy wants to meet face-to-face.

Even though West turns out to be a hunky former SEAL who doesn't seem to mind her cane, her instincts still scream "RUN."

As she resolves to give love a shot, her career-making programming project comes under attack by a hacker. Does she have enough ammunition to fight on both battlefields?

West is haunted by the mission that took the lives of his team. So when he befriends a gamer and former Army ordnance specialist with scars of her own, their connection soothes something in his battered soul.

After the sharp-shooting beauty surpasses his wildest dreams, he's determined to break down the armored panels she's built around her heart. When his own worst fears return, he worries he won't be able to face the coming challenges alone.

With new enemies and old phantoms from their past closing in, can Cam and West find the courage to lower their defenses and heal their wounded hearts with love?

Breaking His Code is the first book in Away From the Keyboard series of explosive military romantic suspense novels. If you like diehard female veterans, sexy cyber romance, and emotional journeys of healing, then you'll love this heartfelt tale of love after war.

One-click **BREAKING HIS CODE** now!

YOU CAN ALSO JOIN my Facebook group, **Patricia's Unstoppable Forces**, for exclusive giveaways, sneak peeks of future books, and the chance to see your name in a future novel!

P.S. Reviews are like candy for authors.

Did you know that reviews are like chocolate (or cookies or cake) for authors?

They're also the most powerful tool I have to sell more books. I can't take out full page ads in the newspaper or put ads on the side of buses.

Not yet, anyway.

But I have something more powerful and effective than ads.

A loyal (and smart) bunch of readers.

Honest reviews of my books help bring them to the attention of other readers.

If you've enjoyed this book, I'd be eternally grateful if you could spend just five minutes leaving a review (it can be as short as you like) on the book's Amazon page.

Turn the page for an excerpt from **IN HIS COLLAR.**

SNEAK PEEK - IN HIS COLLAR

I shouldn't be here.

Nicholas ran a hand through his dark blond locks, tugging on an unruly tuft behind his ear. Flashing his ID at the bouncer—as if the man didn't recognize him—he followed Terrance through the doors of *Bound*.

The heavy, slow beat of the music set his nerves on edge. He'd been all set for the night. A bottle of eighteen-year-old Macallan, greasy pizza, and bitter regrets. Instead, he'd left the bottle unopened on his counter, the pizza order unsent, and his regrets casting a shadow over his soul.

Eight years. She'd been gone for eight years.

Grief faded in the face of the all-too-familiar itch skittering over his skin. *No.* He dipped his hand into his pocket and fingered his eighteen-month chip. Stupid, thinking that a piece of metal could stop the desire to call his bookie, but the smooth pattern under his fingertips calmed the urge.

"Drink?" Terrance gestured to the bar.

"Yeah." Despite the no-alcohol policy the BDSM club maintained, the bar took up half the wall, and lights reflected off dozens of colorful bottles. Nicholas slid his hip onto a stool and scanned the shelves, hoping for a menu or some indication of what the hell he was looking at.

"What'll it be?" The bartender, her black curls tumbling over her right eye in an angular bob, flashed him a smile. "Let me guess. You're new here?"

"That obvious?" Nicholas nodded towards the bottles. "What're my options?"

The woman, whose skin sparkled slightly under the lights, pinned him with a hard stare, and a tiny furrow between her brows begged to be smoothed away. "Trust me?"

"Why not?" He probably wouldn't finish the drink anyway. Though he prided himself on clean eating and only a modicum of alcohol, all he wanted right now was to get plastered, and that wouldn't happen here.

Terrance pulled out the stool next to Nick. "Sorry. The Shibari exhibition on the main stage distracted me. They're having another show in twenty minutes."

"Supposed to be fantastic," the bartender offered as she tipped one of the bottles sending a shot of caramel-colored liquid cascading into the cocktail shaker. "The boss brought in some experts from New York City. One night only." After slamming a glass down on top of the shaker, she nodded at Terrance. "Can I get you something, hon?"

"Bottle of water." The doctor pulled a twenty from his wallet and nodded at Nick. "This cover his too?"

"Yep. Five bucks in change, too."

"Keep it," Terrance said, snagging the bottle of water she'd set in front of him. "I'm going to wander a bit."

As the petite brunette poured Nick's drink into a rocks glass, he glanced around the top floor of the club. Women gathered at a railing, peering down at the stage one floor below. The blonde directly across from him wore a thin, white collar around her neck. A relative newbie looking to play with a willing Dom or

Master. At the other end of the railing, a woman in a bright red corset and spiked heels fingered a black collar with four metal rings attached.

Her Master approached, and she dropped her gaze to the floor. The man held out his hand, and the sub allowed him to lead her away.

"Earth to...um...sir? Let me know what you think." The bartender nudged his drink closer. Nick shook his head to clear the memories that threatened, then turned back to the pretty brunette.

"Not sir. Nick." He didn't want any part of the lifestyle at the moment. Why had he let Terrance talk him into coming out tonight? Rubbing a hand over his chin, Nick met the bartender's gaze.

"You're wearing a Dom's mark." She gestured to the stamp on the back of his hand. "And as your friend paid in cash...I couldn't cheat and snag your name from your credit card."

Shite. Of course. The last club Nick had frequented mandated the use of bracelets and collars for subs and arm bands for Doms. Bound had no such rules, but stamped everyone's hand with either a *D* or an *s* upon entry.

The deep burgundy drink in front of him looked more like cherry soda than anything else, but when he took a sip, the smoky taste of aged scotch mixed with a hint of currant and sage surprised him. "You're not breaking the rules, are you...?" Nick cocked a brow.

"Sofia." She grinned, and the light in her smile reached all the way to her eyes. "No cheating. Experimenting. That's a smoked shrub muddled with half a sugar cube and a couple of secret ingredients. None of which are alcoholic."

"Your recipe?" Nick took another sip and found he didn't miss the buzz of alcohol at all. Something even more intoxicating had caught his eye.

Her head bobbed as she swiped a towel over the bar. "You're

my first victim. I've been begging the bar manager to let me play around with some custom recipes for months. This was a risk, but you looked like you needed something strong." Sofia winked at him. "Plus, I figured if you hated it, I'd finish it for you."

Nick laughed, and something inside his chest threatened to break free. He shouldn't be having fun on the anniversary of Lia's death, but he didn't have much in his life to laugh over these days.

"Hey, you okay?" Sofia leaned forward, resting a hand on his arm. The warmth of her fingers seeped through the expensive material of his shirt. "I feel like we've met before."

"I'd remember you, Sofia," he replied as he slid off the stool. "I'm solid. Thank you for the drink." He downed the last of her "experiment" and set the glass down. "I should go find my friend."

Her lips curved into a gentle frown for a moment until she caught herself. "See ya' around, Nick."

After two interminable hours wandering aimlessly among the crowds and another of Sofia's mystery drinks, Nick ached to go home. The gorgeous bartender provided the only glimpse of light he'd had this evening, but if he went back again, he worried she'd mark him as a creep—or as Nicholas Fairhaven, which might be worse.

The Shibari demonstration left a sour taste in Nick's mouth. The Dom didn't check on his sub often enough, and the woman's right arm had gone numb by the time the demonstration was over. None of the club's Masters walking the floor noticed the sub's fingers turning a darker shade of pink than the rest of her skin, but Nick had. He'd flagged down an employee and suggested ending the demonstration early, but the guy grunted something that sounded like "fuck off" before stalking away.

Now, a headache brewed behind his eyes, and he longed to go home. His text message to Terrance still unanswered, he wandered down a long hallway, hoping to find the man and beg off for the night.

He glanced into a couple of the semi-private rooms. In one, a Domme had her sub on all fours and was whipping his arse with a leather crop. Next door, a woman strapped to a St. Andrew's Cross whimpered as her Master trailed an ice cube over her skin.

Rounding a corner, Nicholas heard Terrance's voice.

"What's your safeword, my dear?"

"Red, sir." A statuesque redhead in a skin-tight dress that looked to be nothing more than a handful of straps artfully arranged reclined on a glossy black table, her arms bound over her head. Terrance dragged a suede flogger over the woman's bare thigh, and she shuddered.

Meeting Nick's gaze, Terrance smiled and waved Nicholas closer. "Melody dear, I came here with a friend. Do you mind if he watches us?"

"No, sir. I'd...like that." The way she batted her eyes as she answered had Nick shaking his head. Though he and Terrance had played together before, taking turns with a delightful sub a few years prior, as part of his recovery, Nick had adopted a rather monkish lifestyle the past eighteen months. As he watched Terrance take control, gently commanding Melody, Nick's heart ached and the emptiness in his soul threatened to drown him. Despite the lack of stimulating conversation, his last sub, Candy, had eased his loneliness for a time. Until suddenly, she hadn't, and he'd turned to horses and blackjack to fill the void. He didn't want to play anymore. He wanted a partner.

After Nick mouthed "have fun," he slipped out of the room.

Despite the club's music, a woman's scream carried into the hall from several doors away.

What the fuck?

The woman screamed again, and the tenor changed to one of pure, unadulterated terror. Nick took off at a run, and three doors down another dark hallway, he skidded to a halt. A burly man clad all in black had a woman pressed against the wall, her wrists pinned in one meaty palm.

"Shut the fuck up," the man growled as his other arm swung up, and something glinted in the spotlights. A syringe.

Nick sprang for the man's arm, but took an elbow to the chin instead. The impact darkened his vision, he stumbled back. Only dimly aware of the woman's whimper, Nick gritted his teeth and blinked hard. The syringe clattered to the floor, and the brute caught his now limp victim in his arms.

Sighting a panic button next to the light switch, Nick rushed forward, slapped his hand over the red knob, set his shoulders, and rammed into the would-be-kidnapper's gut. The unconscious woman slumped to the floor as the two men grappled. "No fucking way you're taking her anywhere," Nick grunted as he landed a punch to the guy's cheek. Two of the club's Masters darkened the door, and the attacker pulled a gun. Nick grabbed his arm, trying to wrestle the pistol from the man's grip.

At the gunshot, his ears screamed in protest, and disoriented, Nick staggered back as splinters fell from the ceiling. Aiming the pistol at the guards, the gunman skirted the edge of the room, slipped out the door, and took off at a run.

Nick crawled over to the unconscious woman as the club Masters chased the gunman. Cradling her in his arms, he smoothed her sleek red hair away from her face. "You're all right," he murmured, though he doubted she could hear him.

"Is that—?"

"Nicholas Fairhaven?" Voices from the hall competed with the ringing in his ears, and Nick looked up to see a handful of patrons snapping pictures of him holding the woman with the syringe on the floor in front of him.

Shit.

Buy In His Collar now!

ACKNOWLEDGMENTS

This book wouldn't be possible without several amazing people.
Wolfe Ross Editing and Jayne Frost edited this book.

My Unstoppable Forces Launch Team provided encouragement, support, and early reading and reviews for All Tied Up For New Year's.

My writing partner, Jayne (who also performed an edit pass for me), talked me down from a couple of tense moments when I didn't think I'd ever get this book done.

My husband shot some pretty amazing photography for teasers for this book.

Until next time!

ABOUT THE AUTHOR

I've always made up stories. Sometimes I even acted them out. I probably shouldn't admit that my childhood best friend and I used to run around the backyard pretending to fly in our Invisible Jet and rescue Steve Trevor. Oops.

Now that I'm too old to spin around in circles with felt magic bracelets on my wrists, I put "pen to paper" instead. Figuratively, at least. Fingers to keyboard is more accurate.

Outside of my writing, I'm a professional editor, a software geek, a singer (in the shower only), and I'm trying to learn how to play guitar. I love red wine, scotch (neat, please), and cider. Seattle is my home, and I share an old house with my husband and cats.

I'm on my fourth—fifth?—rewatching of the modern *Doctor Who*, and I think one particular quote from that show sums up my entire life.

"We're all stories, in the end. Make it a good one, eh?" — *The Eleventh Doctor, Doctor Who*

I hope your story is brilliant.

You can reach me all over the web...
patriciadeddy.com
patricia@patriciadeddy.com

ALSO BY PATRICIA D. EDDY

By the Fates

Check out the By the Fates series if you love dark and steamy tales of witches, devils, and an epic battle between good and evil.

By the Fates, Freed

Destined, a By the Fates Story

By the Fates, Fought

By the Fates, Fulfilled

In Blood

If you love hot Italian vampires and and a human who can hold her own against beings far stronger, then the In Blood series is for you.

Secrets in Blood

Revelations in Blood

Elemental Shifter

Sexy werewolves meet fiery elementals in this modern mix of urban fantasy and paranormal romance.

A Shift in the Water

A Shift in the Air

Contemporary and Erotic Romances

Holidays and Heroes

Beauty isn't only skin deep and not all scars heal. Come swoon over sexy vets and the men and women who love them.

Mistletoe and Mochas

Love and Libations

Away From Keyboard

Dive into a steamy mix of geekery and military might with the men and women of Emerald City Security and Hidden Agenda Services.

Breaking His Code

In Her Sights

Restrained

Do you like to be tied up? Or read about characters who do? Enjoy a fresh BDSM series that will leave you begging for more.

In His Silks

Christmas Silks

All Tied Up For New Year's

In His Collar

Printed in Great Britain
by Amazon